DATE DUE	

Cipher

Also from Larissa Ione

~ DEMONICA/LORDS OF DELIVERANCE SERIES ~
Pleasure Unbound (Book 1)
Desire Unchained (Book 2)
Passion Unleashed (Book 3)
Ecstasy Unveiled (Book 4)
Eternity Embraced ebook (Book 4.5) (NOVELLA)
Sin Undone August (Book 5)
Eternal Rider (Book 6)
Supernatural Anthology (Book 6.5) (NOVELLA)
Immortal Rider (Book 7)
Lethal Rider (Book 8)
Rogue Rider (Book 9)
Reaver (Book 10)
Azagoth (Book 11)
Revenant (Book 12)
Hades (Book 13)
Base Instincts (Book 13.5)
Z (Book 14)
Razr (Book 15)
Hawkyn (Book 16)
Her Guardian Angel
Dining With Angels
Reaper

~ MOONBOUND CLAN VAMPIRES SERIES ~
Bound By Night (book 1)
Chained By Night (book 2)
Blood Red Kiss Anthology (book 2.5)

Cipher

A Demonica Underworld Novella

By Larissa Ione

1001 Dark Nights

EVIL EYE
CONCEPTS

Cipher
A Demonica Underworld Novella
By Larissa Ione

1001 Dark Nights

Copyright 2019 Larissa Ione
ISBN: 978-1-970077-32-2

Forward: Copyright 2014 M. J. Rose

Published by Evil Eye Concepts, Incorporated

This is a work of fiction. Names, places, characters and incidents are the product of the author's imagination and are fictitious. Any resemblance to actual persons, living or dead, events or establishments is solely coincidental.

Acknowledgments from the Author

As always, I went to send out a huge thank you to everyone on the 1001 Dark Nights team. I'm blessed to be working with some of the smartest, savviest, and most supportive women in the business. Thank you, ladies!

Sign up for the 1001 Dark Nights Newsletter
and be entered to win a Tiffany Key necklace.

There's a contest every month!

Go to www.1001DarkNights.com to subscribe.

**As a bonus, all subscribers can download
FIVE FREE exclusive books!**

One Thousand and One Dark Nights

Once upon a time, in the future…

*I was a student fascinated with stories and learning.
I studied philosophy, poetry, history, the occult, and
the art and science of love and magic. I had a vast
library at my father's home and collected thousands
of volumes of fantastic tales.*

*I learned all about ancient races and bygone
times. About myths and legends and dreams of all
people through the millennium. And the more I read
the stronger my imagination grew until I discovered
that I was able to travel into the stories... to actually
become part of them.*

*I wish I could say that I listened to my teacher
and respected my gift, as I ought to have. If I had, I
would not be telling you this tale now.
But I was foolhardy and confused, showing off
with bravery.*

*One afternoon, curious about the myth of the
Arabian Nights, I traveled back to ancient Persia to
see for myself if it was true that every day Shahryar
(Persian: شهريار, "king") married a new virgin, and then
sent yesterday's wife to be beheaded. It was written
and I had read, that by the time he met Scheherazade,
the vizier's daughter, he'd killed one thousand
women.*

*Something went wrong with my efforts. I arrived
in the midst of the story and somehow exchanged
places with Scheherazade – a phenomena that had
never occurred before and that still to this day, I
cannot explain.*

*Now I am trapped in that ancient past. I have
taken on Scheherazade's life and the only way I can
protect myself and stay alive is to do what she did to
protect herself and stay alive.*

*Every night the King calls for me and listens as I spin tales.
And when the evening ends and dawn breaks, I stop at a
point that leaves him breathless and yearning for more.
And so the King spares my life for one more day, so that
he might hear the rest of my dark tale.*

*As soon as I finish a story... I begin a new
one... like the one that you, dear reader, have before
you now.*

Glossary

The Aegis—Society of human warriors dedicated to protecting the world from evil. Recent dissension among its ranks reduced its numbers and sent The Aegis in a new direction.

Fallen Angel—Believed to be evil by most humans, fallen angels can be grouped into two categories: True Fallen and Unfallen. Unfallen angels have been cast from Heaven and are earthbound, living a life in which they are neither truly good nor truly evil. In this state, they can, rarely, earn their way back into Heaven. Or they can choose to enter Sheoul, the demon realm, in order to complete their fall and become True Fallens.

Harrowgate—Vertical portals, invisible to humans, used to travel between locations on Earth and Sheoul. A very few beings can summon their own personal Harrowgates.

Inner Sanctum—A realm within Sheoul-gra that consists of five Rings, each housing the souls of demons categorized by their level of evil as defined by the Ufelskala. The Inner Sanctum is run by the fallen angel Hades and his staff of wardens, all fallen angels. Access to the Inner Sanctum is strictly limited, as the demons imprisoned within can take advantage of any outside object or living person in order to escape.

Memitim—Earthbound angels assigned to protect important humans called Primori. Memitim remain earthbound until they complete their duties, at which time they Ascend, earning their wings and entry into Heaven. Until recently, all Memitim were fathered by Azagoth and raised by humans, but they are now considered a class of angel that can be born and raised in Heaven.

Primori—Humans and demons whose lives are fated to affect the world in some crucial way.

Radiant—The most powerful class of Heavenly angel in existence. Unlike other angels, Radiants wield unlimited power in all known realms and can travel freely through much of Sheoul. The designation is awarded to only one angel at a time. Two can never exist simultaneously, and they cannot be destroyed except by God or Satan. The fallen angel equivalent is a Shadow Angel.

Shadow Angel—The most powerful class of fallen angel in existence, save Satan. Unlike other fallen angels, Shadow Angels can wield unlimited power in all known realms and they possess the ability to gain entrance into Heaven. The designation is awarded to only one angel at a time, and they can never exist without their Radiant equivalent. Shadow Angels cannot be destroyed except by God or Satan.

Sheoul—Demon realm some call Hell. Located on its own plane deep in the bowels of the Earth, accessible to most only by Harrowgates and hellmouths.

Sheoul-gra—A realm that exists independently of Sheoul, it is overseen by Azagoth, also known as the Grim Reaper. Within Sheoul-gra is the Inner Sanctum, where demon souls go to be kept in torturous limbo until they can be reborn.

Sheoulic—Universal demon language spoken by all, although many species also speak their own native language.

Ter'taceo— Demons who can pass as human, either because their species is naturally human in appearance, or because they can shapeshift into human form.

Ufelskala—A scoring system for demons, based on their degree of evil. All supernatural creatures and evil humans can be categorized into the five Tiers, with the Fifth Tier comprising the worst of the wicked.

Chapter One

Blood sport.

Seriously. What the hell?

Lyre watched the spectacle in the arena below, a death match between a fallen angel and a Nightlash demon, the outcome of which would normally be predictable. Fallen angels were a thousand times more powerful than any Nightlash.

But this fallen angel's wings—and source of his mystical powers—had been bound, limiting his abilities, and the Nightlash possessed an *aural*, one of the few reliably lethal weapons against an angel, fallen *or* Heavenly.

The whole thing was so...stupid. The point of this particular battle was to get the fallen angel to cooperate, which he wouldn't be able to do if he was dead.

She gripped the railing so hard her nails left dents in the wood as the Nightlash, his armor dented from Cipher's fists and feet, spun in a blur, slashing at Cipher's bare chest. Cipher fell back with a hiss, and the stench of burnt angel flesh carried to her nose.

"Dammit, Bael," she muttered. "He should have gotten armor too."

The cold air surrounding Bael stirred like the fog off dry ice. He didn't like his decisions being questioned. "Cipher should feel grateful that I allowed him to wear anything at all."

Sure, because jeans were great fighting gear. But they did look amazing on the guy, ripped and stained as they were. Months of captivity read like a horror novel on his pants, but the real story was told in the spark of resistance in Cipher's watchful blue eyes and the cocksure way he carried his lean, muscular body.

He hadn't broken yet, but he would. At least, he would if Bael didn't get him killed first.

Lyre glared at Bael, an ancient fallen angel whose impulsive cruelty and recklessness made him as stupid as it did dangerous. But his chaotic, bloodthirsty nature was exactly what had allowed him to excel as one of Satan's top generals.

"If Cipher dies, you lose your best shot at getting Azagoth's attention," she pointed out.

"Oh, I have The Grim Reaper's full attention." Next to her, Bael smiled coldly, his ebony gaze fixed on the battle below. "And Cipher isn't my only ace, my love."

She forced a smile of her own, but damn, she hated it when he called her, or any female, that. He knew nothing of love. All he knew was hate.

"I'm sure you do," she said, hoping he didn't notice the catch in her voice as Cipher dove to the blood-soaked ground to avoid a swing.

Cipher rolled and swept out his leg, catching the Nightlash behind the knees. Bael nodded in approval as the Nightlash hit the ground hard on his back. The five hundred or so demons in the stands booed. Demons always sided with demons over fallen angels.

Lyre generally didn't give a shit either way, but as Cipher wrenched the *aural* away from the Nightlash, she gave a mental sigh of relief.

Not that she gave a shit about Cipher, of course. She hadn't known Cipher when they'd been Heavenly angels, so she had no prior relationship with him, and while she hadn't been a fallen angel for much longer than he had, she already knew to never get attached to anyone. Sheoul, the demon realm humans called Hell, was a violent place, and no one could be trusted.

So while she couldn't afford to care about Cipher, she did like her job as his handler. She'd balked when Bael had first tasked her with what she'd viewed as a punishment. But it turned out that being assigned to gain Cipher's trust had been a welcome break from her usual duties as Bael's errand girl.

Errand girl.

So mundane. Such a waste of her talents. So not the reason she'd willingly submitted to one of Hell's most powerful warlords after losing her wings.

She wanted revenge on a lot of people, and if Bael played the board right he could make it happen.

But not if he kept sacrificing game pieces.

Cipher plunged the *aural* into the Nightlash's throat, and the crowd erupted in cheers as blood spewed from the demon's mouth. They might root for the demon during the fight, but they were happy to see anyone die.

"He's good," Bael grunted, a rare note of admiration in his hell-smoked voice. "But his hand-to-hand combat abilities are not the skills I need from him." He turned to her, his eyes glinting with black ice, his handsome face and mundane slicked-back chestnut hair concealing the monster that lived behind the mask. "I need what's in his head. I'm growing impatient."

"Impatient?" She snorted. "You once spent an entire century torturing someone for information."

His gaze turned inward, his full lips twisting into a cruel smile as he relived the incident she'd only read about in the history books of Heaven's Akashic Library.

"That was back when the idea of Armageddon was merely a dream," he said. "Now we know we have fewer than a thousand years to prepare for Satan's release from the prison that Revenant, that fucking traitor, put him in."

It was best to not let Bael focus on his hatred for Revenant, especially since, publicly, he professed support for the current ruler of Hell. If he realized he'd spoken aloud, he'd punish her for his own mistake.

The narcissistic asshole.

Quickly, she diverted his attention back to the victor of the fight and gestured to Cipher as he shoved to his feet in the arena below. He'd shown such remarkable resilience no matter what Bael threw at him—extra remarkable, given that with his wings bound, his body's natural ability to rapidly regenerate should have been reduced. But somehow, he healed quickly and maintained his wits.

"Time is short," she admitted. "But Cipher has been here only a few months. It could take decades, even centuries, to turn him. You knew that. It's that very quality, his loyalty to Azagoth, that you desire for yourself. If you want it, you'll have to break him slowly."

"It's not just his loyalty I desire. I need information." He reached out and dragged a finger along the length of her black braid.

She said nothing, gave no reaction as his knuckles brushed the exposed skin of her shoulder, leaving a stinging trail of welts everywhere he touched her. Today was not the day to have worn her favorite camo-print tank top. At least she'd gone for black tactical pants instead of shorts.

"Since you can't seem to get what I need from Cipher, I'm sending in Flail. Maybe she can seduce him into giving me what I want."

Lyre bit back a curse. Of course it would be Flail. That skank always seemed to find a way to screw her.

"She's welcome to *try* to get something from him," she said. "But he hates her for betraying him. If not for her, he'd still be comfy-cozy in Sheoul-gra with his friends and working for Azagoth. The only reason he'll lay his hands on her is to strangle her."

"If he'll give up the information I need, he's welcome to throttle her. Hell, I'd like to see that." He gestured to the guards below, signaling them to take Cipher back to his cell. "Tell him I'll make that deal."

Well, now. Wasn't that interesting? Sycophantic fallen angels like Flail didn't come a dime a dozen, so for Bael to be cool with her death in trade for intel, it meant he was either desperate or Cipher held some seriously important information. She wondered if Cipher would consider the offer. Even under torture, Cipher hadn't spilled anything of use against Azagoth, but he might just change his mind if he were allowed to kill the female who was responsible for every minute of his misery.

Lyre pondered that while she watched as he was escorted, limping, from the arena, blood streaming from dozens of wounds. His blond hair, shorn short when he'd first arrived, hung around his cheeks in limp, damp tangles. He shoved it out of his eyes and scanned the crowd, his gaze rapidly zeroing in and locking with Bael's.

The *fuck you, I'm not dead* message in Cipher's expression was unmistakable.

Lyre's lips twitched in amusement she hoped Bael didn't notice. But Cipher did.

His eyes shifted to her, and was it her imagination, or did he look...disappointed?

Her breath caught. If he was disappointed to see her at this spectacle, it must mean that he was softening toward her. Maybe she could finally get some useful information from him. Something that would earn her Bael's favor and help her get much desired revenge.

It was a small hope, but it was something.

Bael's hand clamped around the back of her neck, startling her so thoroughly she nearly yelped. "You need to step up your game, Lyre. I expected more from you."

Nettle pain stabbed into her skin like a million biting ants. He could turn it off if he desired, and it pissed her off that he chose not to. She'd served him faithfully for more than two years now, and she'd been patient as she waited for the day he fulfilled his promise to her. The day he would deliver pain to those who were responsible for her expulsion from Heaven and the death of the male she'd loved.

But Bael's promise was taking too long.

Snarling, she twisted out of his grip and nearly collided with one of Bael's Ramreel bodyguards. The odiferous, ram-headed beast stomped his hoof in irritation, but she ignored him.

It was a little harder to ignore his barnyard stench.

"Maybe if you allowed me to do what I'm good at," she snapped, "you'd get better results and I'd be closer to getting justice."

"I don't give a hellrat's ass what you're good at." A three-eyed raven landed on the railing, and Bael reached out to stroke his pet's shimmering feathers. "What do I need an expert in demonic history for? *I* lived it. *You* learned it from books written by angels."

She'd explained this to him a million times, so hey, what was one more? "At the Academy of Angels I also studied the various political factions in Sheoul," she reminded him. "Later, I was one of the intelligence department's top analysts. It's why I came to you after I fell. I can help you build alliances with other warlords as we move toward a confrontation with Heaven. I know who supports Revenant and who plots a coup against him to seat themselves or to re-seat Satan—"

Pain went off like a bomb in her head, a sudden crack of agony that made her empathize with broken eggs. But instead of yolk, warm, sticky blood oozed from her nose and ears.

Bael's voice scrambled her brain inside her shattered skull. "You do not speak of such things in the open, stupid whore!"

"I'm sorry, my lord," she rasped, dropping to her knees as the misery wrapped around her entire body and burrowed deep into her bones. She hated submitting to him, hated being so weak and vulnerable, but she'd lived like that in Heaven too. She'd had a lot of practice. "I— I'll do better."

"Yes," he growled, "you will."

He grasped the top of her head and forced her to look up at him as he laughed, his fangs visibly throbbing as he got off on her pain.

And this, she knew all too well, was merely the foreplay.

Chapter Two

Cipher's nightmares had teeth.

Lots of them. Hell, even the dreams in which he was living in a Heavenly palace of crystal featured gaping maws lined with rows of razor sharp fangs. The only difference was that in those dreams, the teeth were beautiful instead of dripping with saliva, blood, and bits of flesh.

And the only thing worse than the nightmares was waking up.

Cipher groaned as he came to, naked except for the threadbare blanket wrapped around him on the glazed-ice floor of the cell he'd called home for...how long now? Six months? Seven? A hundred?

Fuck.

But not to be a total whiner, he did get breaks from the cell. Sometimes he got to visit the Isle of Torture, which was exactly what it sounded like. Lord Bael, the fallen angel who ruled the region, had constructed an island in the middle of a lava river and dedicated it to the art of pain. The question, every time Cipher was put in chains and led from Bael's glacial palace's dungeon to the scorched island, was whether he'd be a participant or a spectator.

Cipher generally preferred being a spectator. But every once in a while Bael would drop him into the arena and force him to fight for his life, and that...that gave him a fucking rush. Who wouldn't love a chance to brush up on fighting skills and let off some steam? Not to mention the fact that his change in status from an Unfallen angel into a True Fallen angel had given him an appetite for dishing out pain to his enemies.

Not that, as both a Heavenly and an Unfallen angel, he hadn't enjoyed serving up some well-deserved death. But now he enjoyed serving his opponents their own innards before they died.

So yeah, the arena gave him a brief taste of pleasure in this realm of perpetual misery. But even during those precious moments of ecstasy, when his opponent grunted in pain or bled from a wound, two voices whispered in his mind.

The first belonged to his buddy Hawkyn, laden with disappointment as he uttered the words Cipher imagined Hawk would say if he knew how much evil was seeping into Cipher's body with every new day spent in Sheoul.

This isn't you. You're decent. Honorable. An idiot, yes, but an honorable one. Fight it, Ciph. Don't give in to evil. You know what it did to Satan. And Lucifer. And my father.

No shit. Cipher hadn't met the first two infamous fallen angels, but he'd worked for Azagoth, the literal Grim Reaper, long enough to have seen what eons of exposure to malevolence did to a person.

And now he could add Bael and his bastard brother, Moloc, to the list of sadistic, evil-ravaged fallen angels he had firsthand experience with.

Which brought him to the second voice that spoke in his head when he was getting off on beating down demons in the arena.

Don't die, Cipher. Don't. Die. If you die in Bael's realm, your soul won't be whisked away by griminions *and taken to Azagoth. It'll be trapped here, where Bael can torture you for eternity in ways you can't even imagine.*

Lyre had told him that, but she was wrong. He *could* imagine it. He'd seen what Azagoth could do to a soul. Still, Cipher would prefer that his soul reside with Azagoth, who was an ally and the father of his best friend, rather than spend the rest of his eternal life with a sadistic motherfucker who hated him.

The sound of approaching footsteps outside his cell brought him to his feet. Maybe it was time for food. Or, more likely, it was time for another round of torture. If he was lucky, the torture would come in the form of his newest handler, a pretty raven-haired fallen named Lyre.

His pulse picked up in anticipation, which was a sad measure of how shitty Cipher's life was; he was actually looking forward to seeing one of his captors. Sure, she was gorgeous, but what intrigued Cipher most was that, unlike everyone else in Bael's realm, she hadn't gone completely rotten to the core with evil. Not yet. Which was awesome, because unlike his two handlers before her, she hadn't strung him up with razor wire and beat the shit out of him. Yes, she'd shoved him into a pit full of demonic piranha once, but only because he'd done the same to her on the first day of her assignment.

It had been his twentieth attempt at escape, and it had gone as badly as the nineteen before, ending at the wrong end of a Darquethoth torturemaster's skinning knife. The weird thing was, Lyre hadn't attended his torture. She never did.

But she'd been at the arena last night for his latest death match. Had she hoped he'd win? Or had she wanted to see him die? She'd looked like she was having fun, in any case.

Gotta love good old family entertainment in Hell. He wondered what the concessions stands served. Probably not popcorn and Red Vines.

The heavy metal lock outside his cell clanked, and the door swung open. He shoved to his feet as the hulking eight-foot tall Ramreel guard moved aside to allow his visitor to enter.

Curiosity veered sharply to rage at the sight of the flaxen-haired fallen angel who stepped inside, her thigh-high leather boots clacking on the floor as she strutted to the middle of the cell.

Flail.

She might have changed her hair color, but the she still reeked of deception. Hatred unlike anything he'd experienced before consumed him, rerouting all rational thought and leaving him with only one goal.

"*You.*" Dropping his blanket, he charged her. "You *bitch.*"

He was going to kill her with his bare hands.

He'd wrench her head from her body and impale it on that shard of ice over there, and then he'd—*holy fuck!*

A red-hot bolt of agony detonated inside his chest, blasting him backward like a rag doll. His spine crunched into the ice-glazed wall, and he crumpled to the floor. The impact shook the massive icicles that hung from the ceiling like monster fangs, and he cursed his impulsive mistake as dozens broke loose and rained down on him.

"Hello, baby," Flail purred. "It's been a while."

"It hasn't been long enough," he growled as he sat up, clutching his throbbing chest and wondering where she'd stashed the sledgehammer. "But remind me, how many months has it been since you got me dragged down to Hell?"

Demons had done the actual dragging, but she'd been the one to call them in when he left the safety of Azagoth's realm, Sheoul-gra, to help Hawkyn's sister kill a seriously dangerous demon. As a wingless, powerless Unfallen angel, he'd been exposed and vulnerable, and Bael's minions had done a grab-and-go. He'd been forced to watch helplessly as his friends ran toward him in a futile attempt to save his dumb ass. Twenty-four hours later, he'd morphed into a True Fallen angel, with fangs, wings, and no hope of Heavenly redemption.

Making it worse, the lone benefit of becoming a True Fallen was the restoration of powers, but because his wings had been bound with enchanted twine, he couldn't access either. He didn't even know what talents he'd gained. Some might be the evil counterpart to their Heavenly versions. Some might be unique to Sheoul. He had no fucking idea.

The most maddening part was how he could sense the power inside him, the strength that ran through him like lit kerosene, but he couldn't touch it. Couldn't bring it streaming to the surface in the form of a weapon or a healing wave or a telepathic conversation. It sat there, frustratingly out of reach, like a donut in the window of a closed pastry shop.

Man, he missed donuts.

"Well?" he prompted. "How many months have I been without donuts?"

"Seven, I believe." She shrugged, and one of her breasts nearly popped out of her tight crimson corset. Why did all fallen angels wear those things?

Not all. Not Lyre.

No, Lyre was all about being ready for battle, from her boots to the dagger holstered at her hip to her sexy BDU pants or cargo shorts that emphasized a seriously perfect ass. And always a tank top. She could have stepped out of an action RPG, like his Mass Effect character come to breathing, beddable life.

If his existence ever stopped sucking long enough for him to get an erection even once, she was going to provide him with some serious fantasy material.

The way Flail used to, before she turned out to be a traitorous evil slutbag.

"Seven?" He gulped a pained breath. "You don't know?"

"Like I keep track." She rolled her eyes. Her traitorous evil slutbag eyes. "You were one of dozens of Unfallen I'm contractually bound to deliver to Bael and Moloc."

The mere names of the twin fallen angels was enough to terrify any sane person, and they weren't a threat to be sneezed at.

But if they were a sneeze, Cipher's former employer was the fucking swine flu.

He allowed himself a dark smile at the knowledge that she was going to die even if it wouldn't be at his hands.

"You know you didn't betray only me," he said. "You betrayed Azagoth."

She tossed her head like a high-strung hell mare. "He's powerless outside of his realm, and I don't plan on returning."

That was where she was wrong. Dead wrong. Azagoth's reach extended far beyond the boundaries of Sheoul-gra. He couldn't leave his realm, but there was no corner of Heaven or Sheoul he couldn't touch. With eons of knowledge and secrets gleaned from the souls he interrogated, he had resources beyond her comprehension.

Not that Cipher would tell Flail that. She'd see for herself when she was pissing in those black leggings at Azagoth's feet and begging for mercy.

"Even if he doesn't kill you, you'll die eventually." He breathed deeply as the pain in his chest eased. "Your soul will belong to him."

"Not if he's no longer in charge of Sheoul-gra."

He barked out a laugh. "No longer in charge? You know something I don't?"

Azagoth had ruled Sheoul-gra for thousands of years, since the day he'd willingly given up his wings to create a holding tank for evil souls that were wreaking havoc on humans. He'd *built* Sheoul-gra and created its specialized demons, *griminions*, from the materials given to him by both Heaven and Sheoul. He wasn't going anywhere.

"I'm sure I know a lot of things you don't." She twirled a lock of hair around her finger. "For example, I know that you're going to give me the list Bael wants."

The fuck he was. The list containing the names and last known locations for all of Azagoth's children, those who didn't yet have angelic powers or knowledge that they were anything but human, was safe on his laptop. Bael might have his computer, but neither he nor his minions had been able to even open the case, let alone access the list inside.

And there was no way he was giving it up to Bael. At least, not while he retained even a sliver of his current self. His fear, his crippling fucking fear, was that he'd succumb to evil and willingly spill all of his knowledge of Azagoth and his realm. Or worse, that he himself would be stupid and arrogant enough to use his knowledge against Azagoth.

"Maybe you could tell me why he wants it," he hedged.

"Does it matter?"

"Well," he said, not bothering to hide his sarcasm, "since I doubt Bael wants the names and addresses of Azagoth's children so he can send them birthday cards, then yeah, it matters."

She thought on that for a moment, toe tapping dramatically. Once upon a time, he'd appreciated her love of theatrics in bed, but right now it was getting on his nerves.

Finally, she pasted on a smile. "Bael is planning to spoil them with ice cream and maybe a movie."

"Real sincere, Flail." He rubbed his sternum absently, the curious tingle there adding to his irritation. "Try again."

"*I'm* not the one named for being a liar."

"Lyre? Kinda random to bring her up, but now that you do, I don't trust her, either. But *she* only shoved me into a pit of flesh-eating demon fish. *You* got me dragged to Hell and destroyed my chances of getting back into Heaven."

"Pfft." She nudged his foot with her toe like one might poke a dead thing they found in the woods. "Why would you want to go back there?"

"Because," he said as he kicked her away, "—and I can't stress this enough—no one tortured me there." And what the *fuck* was up with his sternum? It wouldn't stop aching.

"Give up the list and no one will torture you here either."

Something pinched. Hard. Jerking his hand from his chest, he looked down and drew a startled breath at the weird little ivory disk stuck there, a penny-sized piece of fuckery he was sure couldn't be a good thing.

"What. The. Hell."

"Isn't it pretty? It's an *ascerdisc*. Ever heard of one?"

He had. His friends Hawkyn and Journey had shown him around Azagoth's treasure room, and they'd told him it was a mysterious fallen angel weapon so rare that they believed it to be the only one in existence.

He couldn't keep the stunned note out of his voice. "You stole it from Azagoth?"

"Oh, you simple fool. That's not how they work. The *ascerdisc* in your chest was made from my bones, and I alone can control it. If Azagoth has one, it belonged to another fallen angel." She smiled. "I'll bet everything you think you know about them is wrong. Let's see, shall we?"

Oh, shit. This was not going to be a good time. But hey, if he ever saw Hawk and Journey again, at least he could rub in how wrong they'd been.

Yup, as Hawkyn liked to say, Cipher could see the bright side of anything.

Chapter Three

Most of Journey's thousands of adult brothers and sisters thought that spying on their charges was the worst part of being a guardian angel. Specifically, a wingless Memitim guardian angel, bred to live in the human realm as they worked to earn their wings and a place in Heaven. They'd rather be fighting demons or doing research than hanging out in an invisible bubble while their Primori went about their day-to-day lives. Some didn't like feeling like voyeurs, but most were just bored out of their minds.

For Journey, spying was the *best* part of the job. Depending on who he was spying on, of course. Of his current four Primori, only one kept him entertained. The others, two human scientists who sat around in labs all day, and a werewolf construction worker with no social life, were serious yawners.

But he did have to admit to a twinge of shame for watching Declan as much as he did. The guy was his freaking brother-in-law. Which was actually how he justified staying so close. His sister, Suzanne, would be pissed if he let anything happen to the guy.

But the truth was that Declan fought demons for a living with the Demon Activity Response Team, and there was always shit going on. It was even better than *Live PD*. Much, much higher stakes.

And then there was the fact that his father had ordered him to stay close and listen closer. Azagoth had seen an opportunity to gain intel, and he'd been right. Even informal gatherings of DART members such as the one they were having now yielded tasty nuggets of information.

He braced his hip against a wall and nearly stepped on the ferret that ran under his foot. It chattered at him, and he held his breath as the critter's owner and a founding member of DART looked over from where she was seated at the dining room table with the others. Journey knew she couldn't see him, but some animals could, and that noisy little weasel was clearly one of them.

"Hey, buddy. You need to eat your dinner." Tayla scooped up the animal and set him down in the kitchen of the luxury apartment she shared with her mate, Eidolon. She nudged its dish with her foot and turned to the guys at the table. "Anyone want a beer while I'm up?"

There were three "no's" and a silent "yes" from Journey.

Arik Wagner, husband of Limos, the Horseman of the Apocalypse known as Famine, emphasized his "no" with a shake of his head as he tapped on his phone. "Did I tell you guys that Reaver came by the house last week?"

Declan gave a low whistle. He'd only been introduced to the supernatural world recently, and the newness of it still left him awestruck at times. "Must be weird to have a Radiant as a father-in-law."

"You know what's weird?" Tayla asked. "I knew Reaver back when he was a powerless Unfallen angel working at Underworld General Hospital. Now he and his brother are the most powerful angels in the universe."

Even weirder, Reaver's brother, Revenant, ruled Hell even though he wasn't technically a *fallen* angel.

Arik gave Declan a sideways glance. "My father-in-law might be an angel, but yours is the Grim Reaper. Not sure you want to be calling my situation weird."

Declan laughed. "Yeah, but my father-in-law is relegated to his realm and can't drop in anytime he wants."

"Good point," Arik conceded as he looked back down at his phone. "But Reaver's a great source of intel. When he was at the house he said he'd heard that some fallen angel named Bael is gathering Unfallens."

The very name made Journey bristle. Hawkyn suspected that Bael was behind Cipher's abduction, but they hadn't gathered any proof so far. And the bitch who'd deceived them all in order to gain their trust and get inside Sheoul-gra had disappeared without a trace and with Cipher's laptop.

"Bael?" Kynan Morgan's battle-ravaged voice dipped even lower and rougher. "That's not good."

Arik frowned. "I didn't get a chance to ask Reaver about the guy. Who is he?"

"Bael was one of Satan's most trusted generals." Tayla sank into her seat and wiped her finger over her iPad a few times before spinning it around to Arik. "This is a sketch of him. He and his brother Moloc fell from Heaven and remained loyal to Satan until Revenant and Reaver locked him away. Together, Moloc and Bael control about a quarter of Sheoul."

They also controlled a lot of souls, and Azagoth didn't take kindly to those who denied what rightfully belonged to him. The cold war between Azagoth and the brothers had gone on for over a century, with both sides stepping up their aggressions recently.

"Are they working for Revenant now?" Declan asked. His gaze skipped over to Journey, and Journey swore the guy looked right at him before turning his attention back to Tayla.

"Unknown," Kynan said. "My intel indicates that they've agreed to recognize him as the rightful ruler of Sheoul, so if Bael is gathering Unfallens, he's doing it against Revenant's edict."

Journey had only seen Revenant once, but it had been enough to know that he would be very careful about going against anything the guy said. As a Shadow Angel who had been tutored by Satan literally since birth, he was at the top of the food chain. His power eclipsed even Azagoth's. Only a dipshit who wanted a scythe up the ass would cross him.

"Oh," Arik said as he glanced over at Declan. "Reaver also said something about Bael nabbing an Unfallen who worked inside Sheoul-gra. Thought you might want to tell Suzanne. Sounds like info Azagoth would want to know."

Journey's pulse did an excited little kick. Arik had to be talking about Cipher. Had to be.

Finally, a break.

Declan leaned back in his chair and stretched his long legs out in front of him. "I just hope it's news Azagoth wants to hear. He only yesterday reopened his realm to Memitim and a few Unfallen and fallen angels he trusts, and Suzanne said he's still in a temper over the death of one of his young children inside his realm."

"I can't believe anyone was stupid enough to infiltrate Sheoul-gra and kill a kid right under his nose," Tayla said. "When he finds out who did it..." She let out a low whistle.

Yeah, the general consensus was that Azagoth was going to go supernova on the bastard. All Memitim would. It was just last week that someone had snuck inside Sheoul-gra and slit the throat of a boy who hadn't even grown into his powers yet. He'd been taken from the human realm to a place that should have been nothing but safety, and instead, he'd lost his life within days of arrival.

Journey had no doubt that they'd learn the identity of the perpetrator, but for now he was just going to be happy that he had some information about Cipher.

Feeling hope for the first time in months, he flashed himself to Sheoul-gra's landing pad, and then he found Hawkyn and their brother Maddox exactly where he thought they'd be.

In the kitchen scarfing the Red Devil's Food Cake their sister Suzanne had promised to deliver this afternoon. Maddox had crumbs all over the front of his navy Rick and Morty T-shirt, and Hawkyn had smeared frosting on the sleeve of his leather bomber. Those two didn't need a table, they needed a trough.

"Yo," he called out. "I got a lead on Cipher." He skidded to a halt in front of them as they shoved their faces full of cake.

"Holy shit," Maddox mumbled through frosting. "You serious?"

Journey reached for a plated slice. "I was checking in on Declan while he was meeting with some DART colleagues, and they were talking about the increase in Unfallens being dragged to Sheoul."

Hawkyn drained a can of cola in half a dozen swallows and popped a perfect two-pointer in the nearby garbage pail. "DART is a demonic activity response organization. They fight demons. Why would they even care about angelic issues?"

Maddox gave Hawk a "duh" look. "Maybe because Declan's married to a Memitim?"

"Yeah, I get why *he* would be concerned, but what about the others?"

"Arik was there," Journey explained. "Reaver told him that Bael captured an Unfallen who worked in Sheoul-gra."

Hawkyn let out a nasty curse. "I knew it. That *bastard*."

"Bael?" Maddox let out a low whistle. "No one was tighter with Satan."

"Top tier evil," Hawkyn acknowledged. He turned back to Journey, his emerald eyes bright with hope. "Did Arik say anything else? Did he have a name?"

"No, but it has to be Ciph. No other Unfallen who worked for Father has gone missing."

"That's awesome." Maddox reached for the black leather duster and weapons belt slung over the counter. "Let's get him."

"Easy there, Quick Draw." Hawk shot Mad a "you're kidding, right?" look. "Do you know how big Bael's territory is? Even if we could access that part of Sheoul, we don't know where Cipher's being held." He dug his phone from his jacket pocket. "Although I do have a crude map of Bael's prison region somewhere..."

"You sure Cipher's being held?" Journey hated to even suggest it, but he'd seen what being exposed to evil did to people. "He could be with Bael voluntarily."

The temperature in the room dropped so low that Journey could see Hawkyn's breath as he lifted his gaze from his phone's screen.

"Cipher would never betray us," he said, his voice going as low as the temperature. "If he could be here, he would."

Hawk's faith in his best friend was admirable, but Journey wasn't so sure it was deserved. When an Unfallen entered Sheoul, the act completed his fall from Grace, allowing evil to fully penetrate. No matter how decent Cipher might have been as an Unfallen, evil was now a part of him. His new wings would be formed with it. His powers and abilities would all be tainted by it.

But to what degree? That was always the question when it came to fallen angels. Most had malevolence seeping from their pores and they were giant, radioactive dickbags. But a few, usually those who were only recently fallen, weren't half bad. Maybe if they got to Cipher in time, they could save him from the worst of it. Or at least hold it off for a few centuries.

"Okay, man." Journey held up his hands in a defensive gesture. "Take it easy. I just wanna address the big, awkward demon elephant in the room, you know?"

Hawkyn glared, but a moment later was back on his phone. "I've got the map, and I think I have a file that can help us." He tapped on his phone as he spoke. "Last year Cipher probed the personal networks of about a dozen of Azagoth's enemies to look for back doors into their security systems and tech."

Journey nodded excitedly, knowing where this was going. "I helped him with that. Bael was one of the targets."

"Tell me you guys breached his shit," Hawkyn said.

"We did." Journey grinned at his brothers. "Boys, I think we can help Ciph."

Journey dove into his cake with an enthusiasm that had been missing since Cipher disappeared. They were finally going to help save their friend.

But after seven months in a Hell realm, how much of Cipher would be left to save?

Chapter Four

"Say it, Cipher. Don't make me have to hurt you again."

Cipher's fiery curses didn't melt any of the ice in his cell, but they made him feel better. Flail had spent what felt like hours making him say stupid shit, because if he didn't, she punished him through the bone *ascerdisc* embedded in his skin. Which was seriously gross.

In any case, up until now he'd done what she wanted and said the stupid shit, avoiding major pain. But at some point she was going to stop toying with him and get serious about the torture.

Still, this particular sentence was especially stupid, and he'd initially refused. His chest throbbed like a sonofabitch from that little act of defiance.

"Cipher..."

"Fine." He rolled his eyes so hard it hurt. "My dick is the size of a cocktail wiener."

When she giggled and clapped, he threw his head against the wall and looked up at the remaining hundreds of icicles hanging from the cavernous ceiling, some as big as he was.

They hurt a lot when they fell.

Too bad one didn't fall on Flail.

Carefully, he shifted his weight, keeping his wing anchors from supporting too much weight. The binding rope around the base of his new fallen angel wings, deep inside his back, hurt like hell. Any pressure was agonizing. The worst part about it was that he hadn't even seen his wings yet. Bael had ordered them to be secured before they had a chance to emerge.

"How long did it take you to break, Flail?"

She blinked. "Break? No one broke me. After Heaven rejected me, I entered Sheoul willingly and proudly."

"*Rejected* you." That was too absurd to waste a laugh on. "Next you're going to say you're innocent of whatever got you kicked out."

"I wasn't innocent in the least," she said, her words clipped with irritation. "But it was still bullshit. I mean, so I killed a few humans without permission. So what? Most of them were scum. What happened to me was completely unfair."

"Unfair?" Was she insane? "Killing humans without cause or authorization is the worst offense on a long list of offenses—by far. You broke the number one rule, and you're surprised that you lost your wings?"

She made a sound of disgust. "I understand that I broke the law, but the law is ridiculous. Humans are like an infestation of insects. How can it be wrong to kill them?" He must not have schooled the shock in his expression, because she jammed her fists on her hips and scowled at him. "I'm not alone in feeling that way."

"No shit," he said. "It's kind of why Satan and his cabal of evil assholes were kicked out of Heaven."

"Thanks for the history lesson," she said dryly. "But you're clearly not grasping the size of the anti-human movement amongst Heavenly angels."

"How would you even know?" he shot back. "You've been fallen for what, eight hundred years?"

She eyed one of the icicles above, the pointiest one, and he made a mental note to avoid being under it. "That span of time is but a blink of an eye for angels. You know that. But you're wrong. I lost my wings fewer than three centuries ago."

"Yeah, well, I was in Heaven far more recently than that, and no one was talking rebellion."

Her lips, which had at one time brought him a lot of pleasure, pursed in annoyance. "They wouldn't speak openly of it. Some of the people you think you know the best probably agree with me."

He wanted to tell her how wrong she was, but now that he thought about it, he'd heard stirrings of discontent. Angels of the old guard, those who had been around since before the Earth supported life of any kind, had waited a long time for humans to prove themselves worthy.

Many of those who hadn't supported Satan's rebellion and who had preached patience were beginning to rethink their positions. And younger angels who had come along later in human evolution saw only a species that was destroying itself and the planet they'd been given.

It's like humans are devolving, Tuvol, one of Cipher's oldest friends, had said once. *We had such high hopes for them, but they're a failed experiment. It's time Father ends it. The other living things on Earth will be better without their cruelty and selfishness.*

As shocked as Cipher had been, he'd written off Tuvol's opinion as non-mainstream, shared by an insignificant number of fringe malcontents whose influence was equally as insignificant.

But what if that wasn't true? What if the extremists were growing in number and influence?

"Let's say there are more of you than I think," he said. "What is it they want?"

She stared at him like he was an idiot. "How can you not know? They want the Apocalypse."

Now *that* was worthy of a bark of laughter. "I hate to tell you this, psycho, but Heaven has always been working to prevent the Apocalypse."

Flail kicked his foot again, this time harder. "The Apocalypse is inevitable, Cipher. Just as there are religious demon and human radicals who work to bring about the end days, there are angels as well."

"But the point of delaying it is to allow humans time to perfect their souls." That was the entire argument against Tuvol's "failed experiment" bullshit. Yes, humans were awful and seemed to be regressing, but they learned from the bad times—not the good ones. "To become worthy of the eternal life they'll be gifted with after they've lived several earthly lives and experienced all there is to experience."

She made a gagging gesture. "Ugh. You sound like a fucking textbook. Don't you realize that they will never succeed? Why prolong the agony? If Armageddon kicks off before humankind perfects itself, all human souls will be extinguished."

"Bullshit. When the end of days comes, all good souls will cross over, no matter whether they're perfected or not."

She shrugged. "That's what we're all told, isn't it? Now, if we're done with the theological debate, let's get back to why I'm here." She gestured to him. "Stand and strip."

Talk about a change of subject. "Thanks, but I'll pass."

"When did you get modest?"

He wasn't modest at all. He had a great body and he saw no reason to hide it. But he also saw no reason to comply with this particular demand.

He'd always been bullheaded.

And it was exactly that trait that had gotten him kicked out of Heaven.

"I'm not playing anymore, Cipher." A wave of agony spread from the *ascerdisc*. He clutched at his chest and moaned as blood trickled between his fingers and down his sternum. "Stand up and drop the fucking blanket."

"Fuck. You."

The agony retreated, but what it left behind was worse—a sudden, overwhelming need to obey.

"What—" he breathed as his fingers went to the knot at his hips. "What the hell?"

"That's how the *ascerdisc* works. Obey or suffer."

Growling, he snapped his hand back...and instant agony returned. The trickle of blood from the device became a stream, and a new trickle started from his nose.

"Just drop the blanket, you fool."

Yeah, okay, he was stubborn, but he liked to think he wasn't a total moron. This was a minor battle he was willing to lose in order to save strength for the next one, which would probably have higher stakes. He pushed to his feet and dropped the sucker. The pain faded.

Flail ogled, even though she'd seen him naked before.

"That is definitely no cocktail wiener," she said before letting out a resigned sigh. "Bael sent me to seduce you. But I know how much you hate me. You'll never fall for any of my tricks."

"Duh."

"So I'm going to make you want me."

He laughed. "That will never—" He broke off with a hiss as his body flooded with sexual need that bordered on pain.

"There you go," she murmured, her gaze becoming drowsy, full of erotic promise.

And he knew well that she kept her promises.

Damn her.

Hatred boiled up and merged with the lust burning hotly in his veins. His body wanted to fuck her. His brain wanted to kill her.

"Why—" he gritted. "Why are you doing this?" She could have beaten him with chains, flayed the flesh off his bones, smashed his organs with a sledgehammer, but instead, she was taking the one thing he had left: his free will.

This was so much worse than any torture he'd suffered so far.

"It's all about self-loathing, my boy." She walked toward him, slowly, deliberately, each hip kicking out in invitation. "You're going to fuck me, and you're going to hate yourself later."

"I'll know it wasn't my choice."

"But that won't be true, will it?" She poked one long, black-lacquered nail into the hollow of his throat. "Deep down, you want me with more than just your cock. And that will eat away at you. Which will let evil in." She smoothed her finger down his chest, through the wet blood. "Every day you give in a little more, but with an emotional wound like that? You'll succumb within days and give Bael what he wants."

"Never," he ground out. But each of her words chipped away at his conviction and tapped into his own secret fear.

"You fell for a reason, Cipher. You fell because you have no self-control, especially with females." She used his blood to paint his skin, and revulsion started to swallow the runaway lust. "You know that if you give in to me now, you're still the same piece of shit you always were, no matter how hard you tried to get back into Heaven."

"Bitch," he hissed. His fangs throbbed with the desire to rip out her throat, but his cock was throbbing for an entirely different reason.

Dropping her hand, she palmed his shaft, and he nearly jumped out of his skin. He stumbled backward out of her grip, and pain crushed his body in a vise of invisible pressure.

"When you resist my order, you suffer. Come to me and there will be only pleasure."

"No." He doubled over and shouted as another round of agony shredded him.

He'd been tortured on a weekly, and sometimes daily, basis since he'd been dragged here. He'd never been close to breaking. But Flail was somehow doing what the others couldn't. She was ripping beyond his flesh and into his soul.

"How?" he rasped. "How are you doing this?"

"We all have superpowers." Her hand came down on his neck, and no matter how hard he tried, he couldn't move. "Why do you think I'm called Flail? It's because my special power, the one that makes me indispensable to anyone who pays me enough, is that little thing buried in your chest. With it, I can use my thoughts like a whip, flaying emotions open."

Her superpower was horrific. Cipher had no idea what his unique fallen angel power was yet, but he hoped it was just as nightmarish.

And then, he swore, he'd use it to kill Flail.

Chapter Five

Cipher's shouts of agony echoed in the dark halls as Lyre hurried toward his cell. The tower guard said Flail was with him, but if that were true, why would Cipher be in pain? She'd been sent to seduce him, not torture him.

Unless...

Shit.

She started past the cobra-faced guard at the cell door, but the big asshole blocked her. "Sssorry. Flail gave ordersss to not allow anyone in."

"I'm not anyone," she gritted out. "I'm his handler, and I outrank Flail in this."

The guy's slitted eyes narrowed even more in confusion, but he still shook his three-horned, hooded head. On the other side of the door, Cipher moaned. Time for a different tack.

Summoning every ounce of power she could muster, she used her one major play and dematerialized into a wisp of gray vapor. In her smoky form she could squeeze through any opening, and the keyhole was just perfect.

She heard the guard's shout of "Hey!" as she slipped inside the cell and rematerialized.

When she'd fully formed, her jaw dropped at the sight of Flail, standing near the center of the small room like a dominatrix, her spike-heeled boots digging into the ice, her arms crossed under her bare breasts. On the floor, puddled like blood, was her corset.

Cipher's glassy gaze jerked over at Lyre as he stood slumped against the icy wall, one hand clutching the *ascerdisc* in his chest. Fury knotted in her own chest as blood ran in thick streams from the device and from Cipher's nose and mouth.

"Bitch!" Without thinking, she slammed an invisible fist of power into the other female's gut, knocking her off her feet and into the remains of a giant fallen icicle behind her. "How dare you torture him."

Flail laughed, flipping to her feet as if Lyre's power punch had been a mere slap. To add insult to injury, Flail shot her a mocking smirk that all but screamed, *Your powers are feeble and you're a pathetic excuse for a fallen angel, and everyone knows it.*

So embarrassing.

"I'm not torturing him." Flail curled her finger at Cipher in a come-here gesture. "He's torturing himself." With a pained hiss, he staggered a couple steps closer to Flail, his hands clenched, rage burning in his eyes. Even his erection, engorged and pulsing with thick veins, seemed angry. Impressive, but angry. "The more he resists, the more it hurts."

"He's not torturing himself and you know it. You're forcing him into it." Lyre cursed. "This is sinister, even for you."

Flail made a sound of disgust. "Such a human thing to say. Next you're going to tell me that this is mind rape." She waved her hand dismissively. "Or rape rape. Whatever."

Well, yeah, technically...

As a fallen angel who had allowed the malevolence of Sheoul inside her, Lyre should embrace all acts and all things evil. But every once in a while, like now, her past and her memories rose up, all inconvenient and shit.

Her ex had been a vigilante of sorts, a demon who'd put his ability to cause nightmares to good use. Anyone who harmed others could find themselves victims of his gift, but rapists had been his favorite targets. He'd have *paid* to haunt Flail's dreams until she went insane.

Lyre couldn't haunt Flail's dreams or drive her insane, but she could put a boot up the skank's perfect ass.

"Get out, Flail." She sent a mental flare at the door, and it creaked open. "He'd rather die than screw you, so this is pointless."

Ignoring her, Flail again gestured to Cipher, inviting him closer. He snarled, his hatred hanging in the frosty air with his breath. But he shuffled toward her, his efforts to resist making his steps jerky and uncoordinated.

Son of a bitch. "I'll call the damned guards," Lyre ground out.

"And you'll answer to Bael," Flail shot back. "He ordered me here."

As a baby fallen angel with weaker powers than most, Lyre was always outranked by every fallen angel she encountered, including Flail. But not here. Not as long as Cipher was in her charge.

Lyre came at Flail, ready to take the skank down with her bare hands. She might be pathetically weak when it came to angelic powers, but she'd spent a lifetime training in physical combat to help make up for her lack of supernatural ability.

"Bael ordered you to seduce him," she said, halting at the very edge of the other female's personal space, "but he ordered me to train him and care for him, and I say he's had enough."

Flail's jaw tightened, her lips mashing into an angry slash, and Lyre summoned power to have at the ready if the other female struck out. Lyre was hopelessly outgunned and outclassed by Flail, but within the confines of the power-dampening cell where only low-level abilities could be used, Lyre could hold her own enough to avoid a serious ass beating.

Plus, she had a really sharp dagger at her hip.

"I'll leave," Flail said in a shockingly peaceful capitulation, "but only because you ruined the mood." She leveled a warning look at Cipher. "I'll be back tomorrow, and we will finish what we started. But your handler's little stall tactic is going to cost you. We're gonna do all of this again...but we'll do it in the arena in front of an audience."

Flail flicked her wrist, and the *ascerdisc* tore out of Cipher's chest with a wet, ripping sound. He grunted and clutched at the bleeding wound as she stalked out of there, not even bothering to take her corset. No surprise. Flail had always been an exhibitionist.

Which was why she was probably already drooling over tomorrow's arena sex show starring Cipher.

For some reason, the idea repulsed Lyre in every way.

She'd attended a lot of Bael's erotic displays—he used the arena to host both pain and pleasure, and if they happened at the same time, even better. And she'd seen Cipher in the arena, fighting battles that could have killed him. But this would be a fight he couldn't win, and death might actually be kinder.

After closing the door, she turned back to Cipher, who watched her with wild eyes, a wounded predator, in pain and more dangerous than ever.

"Let me heal you." Like all her abilities, her healing power was limited in scope and strength, but she could at least take the edge off and jumpstart the process.

He bared massive fangs dripping with his own blood. *"Don't touch me."*

Of all the times she'd seen him following a death match, or torture, or forced hard labor, he'd never looked like this. Exhausted, yes. Bleeding and barely conscious, sure. Trembling and puking, yeah, once or twice. But no matter how battered he'd been, defiance had burned in his eyes. That same unyielding hatred still smoldered there, but now it shared space with doubt. And maybe a little anxiety.

Flail had gotten to him. She was famous for it. But what deep, emotional scar had she ripped open to do it? Cipher wasn't going to survive the arena mentally intact, was he? He'd come out of it as evil as any fallen angel. And then he'd give Bael what he wanted, and Flail would take the credit.

No way. Lyre was tired of waiting to get back at her enemies. She needed this win, and she needed it badly.

"Listen to me," she said as she kicked Flail's corset into a corner. "Flail is going to destroy you in the arena—"

"Never," he spat.

His fire was magnificent, but fires could be put out.

"You know it's true, Cipher." She met his tortured gaze, hoping he'd recognize her genuine concern. He just had to mistake concern for her own situation for concern for his. "You *know* it is. She's going to crack the shield you've got around yourself, and evil is going to pour in and turn you into someone your friends and family won't recognize. And then you'll willingly give up the list Bael wants. But if you give *me* the list, you won't have to go through the hell Flail will put you through. You can hold on to your sanity and yourself for a while. Let the effects of being in Sheoul seep into you gradually instead of pouring in like a dam breaking."

"You think I'm stupid?" he rasped. "You don't give a shit about me. You just want to deny Flail a victory while scoring one for yourself." He inhaled a gurgling breath, his fingers tightening around his gaping chest wound where the *ascerdisc* had been. "And fuck you for making sense." He spat blood onto the floor, where it froze instantly, little drops of color on a canvas of white. "Is that how it went down for you?"

"I wasn't forced to give up anything, if that's what you're asking."

Nope, she'd entered Sheoul with a heart full of screw-you-Heaven enthusiasm. She'd expected evil to take her immediately given that she'd come here of her own free will. Instead, she could barely feel the slow creep of it and sometimes she wished it would happen faster. She'd love to be devoid of empathy. Too much of that crap got you in trouble. Having her own emotions sucked enough as it was. Having to feel for others bordered on overwhelming.

It was why she tried to avoid being anywhere nearby when Cipher was being worked over by torturemasters. It was also why she interfered with said torture as often as she could without looking suspiciously sympathetic. She wasn't squeamish; some people deserved what they got. But during the months she'd spent with Cipher she'd grown to realize that he didn't deserve any of this. The most offensive thing she could find about him was that he liked black walnut ice cream when everyone knew rocky road was the best.

"What about Bael?" He made a gesture that encompassed the glazed ice walls of his cell. "Did he lock you up in the Hellton hotel?"

Lyre almost laughed. If Cipher thought this was bad, he should see the prison where Bael kept the people he *didn't* want to work for him. His true enemies. People who he thought might have slighted or cheated him. People who looked at him the wrong way. The suffering that radiated from the mountain complex fueled entire villages of demons who thrived on the pain of others.

This, the Hellton, as Cipher called it, was downright luxurious in comparison.

"I was never imprisoned," she said, surprised she hadn't told him this before.

They'd talked a lot over the last couple of months, keeping the conversation light as she tried to pry information out of him about Azagoth's realm. Cipher had always deftly shifted the topic away from Sheoul-gra, but in truth, she hadn't minded. She'd been stuck in Bael's territory for years, prevented from leaving by a magical barrier that wouldn't allow her to flash, walk, or take a Harrowgate out. Cipher's stories had given her a tiny sense of freedom in a place where all she knew were shackles.

"I knew of Bael because I'd studied him as an angel," she continued. "I came to him for employment. Now, let me heal you."

He backed up so fast he hit the wall. "I said no."

"You've let me do it before."

His gaze dropped to his erection, just for a second, and her heart skipped a beat. He'd been naked in front her before, but he'd never been...aroused. Was that Flail's angle? Had he been traumatized sexually and she was trying to exploit his pain?

As an angel Lyre would have proceeded from here carefully, with tact and sensitivity. As a fallen angel she didn't have to do any of that. Hell, she could use that little suspected tidbit of information like an instrument of torture the way Flail seemed to be.

She chose to just be blunt. "Is it sex? Is sex your trauma? I wouldn't have guessed that."

"What? Are you kidding?" He looked horrified by the very thought. "Sex is awesome. I just don't want to have sex with *her*. Talk about trauma." He glanced down at his erection again. "But this won't go away, and my blood...burns."

"Oh." Well, this was awkward. "Um...I'm not entirely sure how Flail's ability works, but I think it takes a couple of hours for the pain to subside." Her gaze fell to his hips, where the thick column of engorged flesh curved upward, the glossy tip nearly touching his hard abs. Sweet baby Lucifer, that was impressive. "Or, you could, ah..."

Her cheeks flushed with heat, which was ridiculous, given that she was a couple of centuries old and a fallen angel. She'd watched orgies before, and she couldn't tell Cipher to jerk off?

I so want to see that.

The heat in her face spread to her breasts and pelvis, and she shifted uncomfortably.

"I could what?" He leveled his sharp gaze at her, so intense it took her breath. All his focus was on her. He didn't even seem to be in pain anymore. "I could..." He grasped his shaft, his long fingers wrapping around the thick length. "Take care of it myself?" His fist made a slow pass from the head to the base and back up, and her throat clogged with lust. "Or I could fuck you instead?"

"*Of course not, you worm!*" she said. Silently. In her head. Where Cipher didn't hear it.

Suddenly, he was on her, knocking her back against the door.

She hadn't even seen him move. Her first instinct as he bit into her throat and pressed that enormous erection into her belly was to hit him so hard that even the wings he'd lost would feel it. But when the erotic purr in his chest reached her ears, her body betrayed her.

Months of watching this magnificent creature perform in the arena and stand up to every form of torture thrown at him had put the tiniest chip in the wall she'd erected when she'd lost everything and everyone she'd loved. On the day she'd lost her wings, she'd sworn off love and friendship, tenderness and compassion, and then she'd let evil in, hoping it would fill the empty space inside. Her anger had been, and still was, a shield, protecting her from the cruel reality in which she now lived.

But now, for the first time since she'd fallen, there was a pleasant distraction from the perpetual misery of Sheoul. A distraction who, as coincidence would have it, could help her get revenge.

You need to step up your game, Lyre. I expected more from you.

Bael's words from yesterday in the arena rang in her ears. Shuddering, she clung to Cipher, her nails digging into his rock-hard biceps as if holding him close would block the memory of Bael showing her how much more he expected by chaining—literally chaining—her to his side until this morning. She'd witnessed how he did everything from getting a blow job to taking a shit to skinning an Oni demon alive, so yeah, she saw what happened to those who disappointed him. He didn't handle failure well.

And she had a head full of disturbing memories to process.

Buck up, girl. You can dissect your trauma later. You're working with a ticking clock right now.

She had to get Cipher to give Bael what he wanted, and she had to do it before Flail did it. Because even if Cipher didn't break in the arena, he *would* break eventually. Everyone did. The question was who got credit for it.

Lyre *needed* the credit. Maybe Bael would finally give her the freedom to leave the realm now and then.

Resolved to this course of action, which really wasn't a hardship, she let her head roll to the side so he could deepen his bite, and the rush...oh, yes, the rush was incredible. She'd never been fed on before, had never had anyone ask. No one wanted to feed on a weakling like her. And as a weakling, she didn't even need to feed much. When she did, she fed from humans after being escorted to the earthly realm by other fallen angels who never seemed happy to have to babysit.

During the time she'd been Cipher's handler she could have taken his vein at any time. It hadn't even occurred to her.

Now it was on her to-do list.

Adrenaline rushed through her veins like erotic fuel as Cipher's lips and tongue ravaged her neck. *More of this.* She needed much, much more of this.

Heart pounding so hard Cipher surely must have felt it against his teeth, she slid her hand between their bodies. His warm skin twitched as the backs of her fingers slid across his steel-hard abs, and his breath hitched as her thumb brushed the underside of his shaft.

Her own breath lodged in her throat. She'd never done this before. She and Dailon had been interrupted before they could consummate their love on the physical plane.

Anger at the stupid sentimental glitch roared back, and she roughly took Cipher's cock in her palm. There was nothing to wait for. No prince in angelic armor was going to sweep her into the pillowy embrace of his wings and gently take her maidenhood.

She lived in Hell now. Gang rape or having her virginity sold to the highest bidder for use in some sort of power spell were the more likely scenarios if it ever got out that she was a virgin. She might as well make it happen on her own terms and now was as good a time as any.

Besides, it was only a matter of time before Bael forced her into his bed. Honestly, she couldn't believe he hadn't already.

She squeezed Cipher's shaft, and his gasp of pleasure created an unexpected throb of need deep in her belly.

Stop it.

This was a task. A means to an end. Not a meaningful exploration of her sexuality or some crap.

Oh, but it felt so good.

She squeezed again, adding a slow pump of her fist. Cipher shuddered and rocked into her hand.

A low moan dredged up from his chest as he lifted his head from her throat. "Hurts," he whispered.

She froze, then hastily released him. "I'm sorry—"

"No." His big hand closed around hers and guided it back to his shaft. "Not that." He shuddered again. "That is the only thing that feels good. The only thing in...months."

Sadness mingled with the pain in his voice, and her heart clenched.

No. No clenching of hearts. She was doing this for a purpose.

If she gave Cipher what he wanted, maybe he'd give her what she wanted.

Information.

And, of course, an orgasm.

* * * *

Pain. There was so. Much. Pain.

Even with Flail gone, Cipher's pain was still crippling. It was as if every cell was being alternately crushed then sliced, cycling over and over, with breaks only when he'd willingly moved closer to either Flail or Lyre. Resisting meant that someone dialed up the pain intensity.

But worse than the pain was the desire. The ball-throbbing, dick-tingling, soul-crushing desire to bury himself first in Flail, and now Lyre.

At least Lyre hadn't betrayed him. He didn't completely hate her. And she was hot.

He'd fucked worse.

Probably shouldn't say that out loud. Or think on it too much. Didn't say anything good about him, that was for sure.

Whatever. He was just glad Lyre was here instead of Flail.

How had Lyre gotten in here, anyway? He hadn't seen the door open.

And why the fuck was he thinking about random shit when he should be concentrating on how Lyre's hot blood circulated through his body and her warm hand pumped along his shaft, the only real heat he'd felt since he'd been dragged to Sheoul. It spread across his skin and into his muscles all over his body, and for the first time in forever, misery wasn't the only thing he was feeling.

"Just like that," he rasped as he thrust into her grip.

He wanted to haul her legs up around his waist and take her, right against the door. She'd let him; he could tell by the way she rocked into him, the way her breathing came fast and hard, the way the scent of her arousal wrapped around him like satin. But then she did some kind of twisty thing as she squeezed him from the base of his cock to the head...and he was done.

He threw his head back and shouted as the climax hit him, a giant, rolling wave of pleasure that, for the briefest moment, made him forget everything shitty in his life. More waves followed, weaker, just lapping at his pleasure centers as he came down.

Then someone in a nearby cell screamed, jolting him out of his bubble of bliss and reminding him where he was. Reminding him that pleasure was nothing but an illusion in Bael's prison, a sick joke, a fleeting sliver of time meant to make you hate normal life even more.

God, he hated it here. This was why few Unfallen angels willingly entered Sheoul to complete their fall from grace. Most of them lived a nomadic life, constantly fleeing those who would capture and drag them into Sheoul, just as Cipher had done. He'd spent a couple of decades on the run, hiding in the human realm in the guise of a homeless man, until he'd run into Hawkyn.

Unlike the last time he'd seen Hawkyn, the Memitim hadn't tried to kill him for what Cipher had done to his Primori. Instead, Hawk had offered him sanctuary. Well, he'd offered it after an epic battle in which they'd beaten the shit out of each other in a good old-fashioned fistfight.

Life had been good in Sheoul-gra. He'd rarely had to leave, and when he did, he was usually with powerful friends.

Unfortunately, he'd let down his guard. He'd taken one too many risks, had gotten too far from his friends during a battle, and now he was paying for his mistakes.

He might be reckless, but he wasn't an idiot. He knew this could only go one of two ways. He'd either give in and join Bael's team, or he'd die an agonizing death, only to be fully conscious moments later as his soul found itself at Bael's mercy. Would Bael use it as a plaything? Perhaps trap it inside Cipher's preserved body, put on display while he slowly went mad? Or maybe Bael would keep it as an offering to Satan on the day the King of Demons was released from his prison.

Cipher knew which option was the most likely. Even now he could feel evil seeping into his very cells, darkening his outlook, his sense of humor. Oh, sure, there was always a chance that he could escape and get back to Sheoul-gra, but the reality was that he had only one choice to make.

Pledge fealty to Bael now...or pledge fealty to him later.

Either way, Cipher would give up the list and betray everyone he cared about.

They don't care about you. Flail's voice rang in his head, tapping into his fears. *You've been gone too long. They think you've gone to the dark side already. They've given up.*

No way. They hadn't. They wouldn't. If he could get out of here, they'd welcome him back in Sheoul-gra.

He just needed a plan. A way to contact them.

But to contact them, he'd need his computer. To escape he needed his fallen angel powers. To get his fallen angel powers he needed his wings to be unbound.

There was only one way that was going to happen. He had to give

Bael what he wanted.

The scream rang out again, the prod he needed to get his shit together.

Awkwardly, he stepped away from Lyre, grabbed his blanket, and used it to clean up. "Uh, sorry..." He stopped himself before he said anything else. Why should he apologize? Lyre was his fucking captor. Well, she was employed by his captor, anyway.

"Did it help?" She sounded breathy. Turned on. And despite the fact that he'd just come and he was in a prison in Hell's asshole, he started to get hard again.

"Did what help what?"

She huffed as if he was a complete idiot. "Is the pain gone?"

"Oh. Yeah." But he wasn't sure if he felt better thanks to the nourishment her blood gave him or because of the sex. Maybe both.

He looked down at his chest. Blood still streaked his skin, but the *ascerdisc* wound had sealed and was only a little tender. His wings still hurt, strangled by ensorcelled rope, but that was nothing new.

She started toward him. "Cipher—"

"Ooh, hey, watch your step."

She did a jaunty little hop to avoid slipping on the result of her hand action, and he hid a smile at the way her cheeks turned pink. "Thanks."

"Don't thank me. I warned you before I had a chance to consider how hilarious it would be if you fell in my jizz." Why *had* he warned her, anyway? Should have let her break her ass on the ice.

But it was such a nice ass.

"You know tomorrow's going to be worse, right?" she asked, sounding a little flustered. "Flail is probably drafting invitations right now."

She's going to crack the shield you've got around you, and evil is going to pour in and turn you into someone your friends and family won't recognize. And then you'll willingly give up the list Bael wants. But if you give me the list, you won't have to go through the hell Flail will put you through. You can hold on to your sanity and yourself for a while. Let the effects of being in Sheoul seep into you gradually instead of pouring in like a dam breaking.

As much as Cipher hated to admit it, Lyre's words made sense. And if he'd been here for seven months, like Flail said...yes, this might work.

He tossed the blanket aside. "If I give Bael the list, he'll unbind my wings, right?"

"That's the deal."

"Then bring me my laptop." He paused. "And some clothes. Real clothes. And a shower would be great."

Lyre jerked like she was a marionette and someone had yanked her strings. "Are you serious?"

"I'm covered in blood and I'm naked. What do you think?"

"No, I mean the list." Her silver eyes were wide, glinting with surprise. "You're willing to give Bael the names he wants?"

Hearing her say it out loud made his gut churn. If he was right about this, he could buy time to escape without anyone getting hurt. If he was wrong, Azagoth's wrath would make Bael's cruelty seem downright merciful.

And so, with a deep breath and a silent prayer to anyone who would listen, he nodded.

"Yeah," he growled. "I am."

Chapter Six

"Ever seen the inside of a soul?"

Azagoth frowned at the speaker over the rim of his highball glass filled with Scotch. "You're kidding, right?" He lowered the glass to his desktop. "You're asking me, the Grim Reaper, a fallen angel who hasn't found a new thing to do with a soul in at least two centuries, if I've ever seen what's inside one?"

Jim Bob, an angel whose real name and identity Azagoth didn't know, shrugged, making the hem of his hooded black robe whisper against his boots. "Supposedly, most souls are filled with light. But what about the souls you keep in the Inner Sanctum?"

This was a weird conversation, but Azagoth couldn't work up the energy to be annoyed by something so minor. Not when *big* shit was going on all around him. Big enough that he'd been scattered and sleepless and distracted for days.

Last week, one of his sons, a boy barely in his teens whom Azagoth had only just met, had been murdered inside Sheoul-gra.

Inside Sheoul fucking Gra.

The bastard responsible for Niclas's death hadn't yet been identified, but he—or she—would be. Azagoth wouldn't rest until he knew who had dared to kill one of his children inside his own realm and right under his nose.

One thing of which he was certain: whoever it was, they weren't working alone.

Three of his grown children, trained, powerful Memitim, had also been slaughtered recently, and just this morning he'd learned that, without a doubt, the deaths were connected.

The remains of the demon who'd delivered the message were still splattered on the wall, and his soul was in Hades's capable, cruel hands.

That demon's soul was definitely not brimming with light.

"Most of the souls I deal with are full of blackness," Azagoth replied. Since not all demons were evil, some didn't possess a dark inner void, and a rare handful even radiated light.

Jim Bob walked slowly around the office, his gaze settling on the splatter. "When a good soul full of light is destroyed, the light returns to the Creator unless the soul is trapped, devoured, or used as fuel for a spell. What happens when an evil soul full of darkness is destroyed?"

Azagoth propped his hip against his desk and relaxed although, as always, he kept his powers locked and loaded. Jim Bob was a prime source of Heavenly intel, but he was also an angel. Which meant he could never be fully trusted.

"Same, basically," Azagoth said. "The dark void inside a soul is fuel for a soul-eating demon. But if I destroy a soul, the darkness returns to Satan and makes him more powerful. That's why so few have the power to destroy souls and why I don't do it on a whim." He'd also signed a contract stating he'd pay a hefty price for every soul he destroyed, and that price generally wasn't worth it. Very little was worth giving up a measure of his power or a slice of his realm. "Why the sudden interest in the internal plumbing of a soul?"

Jim Bob swung slowly around, his expression, while always serious was downright grim. "There are rumblings of a plot to free Satan from his prison. I wonder if enough souls were destroyed if he'd gain the necessary powers required to escape."

Azagoth studied Jim Bob's carefully schooled features but, as usual, there was nothing there to read. Still, his question wasn't an idle one; he was probing Azagoth's feelings on the matter. Maybe even his involvement.

"Possibly," Azagoth mused. "But it would take hundreds of years even for *me* to destroy that many souls. By then Satan most likely would be free. According to prophecy, of course."

"Of course." Jim Bob casually waved his hand in front of the fire as he spoke, but if he was looking for heat, he'd have to go elsewhere. Azagoth's fireplace was as cold as his heart and it had been since the day Lilliana walked out on him. "Have you heard any of this talk?"

That *talk* was what got the demon in the corner all kinds of dead.

Azagoth had known there were multiple plots afoot to rescue Satan, and now he knew that he, himself, was central to many of them.

His children's deaths were a message: help us, or else.

Azagoth had a scythe full of "or else" for every motherfucker responsible, but he wasn't going to let Heaven in on this. The less they knew about the pressure being placed on him to back the *#FreeSatan* cause, the better.

They actually had a fucking hashtag.

What the Free Satan movement didn't have was a single leader to bring cohesiveness. The most powerful demons and fallen angels in Sheoul were all campaigning for followers who could get behind their unique visions for making Hell great again.

And they all seemed to think Azagoth's help could be bought.

Or compelled.

He waved his hand in a dismissive gesture. "As long as Satan is imprisoned there will be talk of breaking him out. When he was free someone was always plotting his demise. It's the circle of life. I wouldn't worry."

Jim Bob snorted. "You have more important things to worry about than the End of Days?"

The lives of his children and his mate were more important, so...yes.

Especially now that Lilliana was coming home. Ares's child just needed to hurry the fuck up and be born. He had no idea why Lilliana had insisted she be there for the birth, but by Satan's balls, it felt like the Horseman's mate had been pregnant for years.

Lilliana had been gone for nine months now, and every single day, every single minute, had been torture. Not that he had anyone to blame but himself. It had taken him a long time to realize that, but now that he had, he'd been working on becoming the male Lilliana deserved.

"...and then I was abducted by alien angels from an alternate universe," Jim Bob said. "They gave me pizza before the anal probe."

"What?" Azagoth snapped, re-focusing his thoughts. They went to Lilliana at the most inappropriate times. She really needed to come home. Fucking Ares. "Did you say something about pizza?"

Jim Bob rolled his eyes. "Pizza? *That's* what snapped you out of your funk? Not the alternate universe or anal probe?"

Azagoth shoved away from his desk. "I'm hungry, not horny." Actually, that wasn't entirely true. Sure, he could go for a couple of large pepperonis. He hadn't eaten in days. Hadn't eaten much at all since

Lilliana left.

But he really was horny as hell. It had been eons since he'd gone this long without sex, but more than that, he'd never gone this long without Lilliana.

In the past, he'd had an endless parade of sexual partners. Demons had thrown themselves at him and Heaven had kept him supplied with angels to make baby Memitim with, so no, there'd been no shortage of sex. Which was fortunate because, as his fallen angel Chief of Operations, Zhubaal, liked to say, "There's nothing more frightening than the Grim Reaper when he's horny."

Yup, he was horny as fuck. But for all the evil that ran through his veins, he'd never even so much as glanced at the females who tried to seduce him while Lilliana was away. And there had been thousands, most of them demons who wanted to trade sex for mercy. But mercy wasn't his thing, and he'd laughed as his *griminions* whisked them away, ushering their souls to their new, nightmarish digs.

He'd never been tempted, not once. Even his evil side wouldn't betray Lilliana for a blow job from a succubus.

But his evil side did enjoy the game. It enjoyed toying with the angels and fallen angels who came into his office thinking that with Lilliana gone they could get their claws into him.

Jim Bob's fingers snapped in front of his face. "Yo. What the fuck, man? Put your horns and fangs away. And stop snarling. Makes my wings itch."

Azagoth blinked as he once again climbed out of the mire of his own thoughts. His body vibrated with a dark lust as the memories of toying with prey collided with a sexual awareness that burned deep in his muscles. Warmth crept into his cold flesh, and his cock, already excruciatingly hard, began to throb to the beat of his pulse.

His pulse.

Holy hell, his heart had started beating again.

"Lilliana," he breathed, joy taking his breath as her presence filled his soul. "She's here. She's home."

Another spike of awareness pierced him, a powerful energy signature he'd never felt before.

What the fuck?

A possessive, smoky growl rattled his chest, and his hackles rose with his wings. Someone else was here. Someone crazy strong.

Lilliana wasn't alone.

Chapter Seven

Lilliana inhaled a shaky breath as she stood on the portal pad inside Sheoul-gra, the symbols engraved into the stone glowing hotly. A breeze swirled around her, rattling the leaves on the perpetually blooming citrus trees and bringing their tangy and sweet scents to her nose. Grassy lawns stretched for acres, broken by babbling streams and worn paths—and the occasional ancient Greek column or demonic statue that rose into the featureless gray sky.

Several yards away, a fountain that once ran with blood splashed crystal water onto pavers leading to outbuildings that housed dozens of Unfallen angels and Memitim. And beyond the fountain, Azagoth's palace towered over all, its pale walls gleaming.

Relief sifted through her, temporarily replacing her nervousness. The realm was attuned to Azagoth's moods, and she wasn't sure what she'd have done if she'd come back to find the kind of decay and evil that had once held court here.

The Grim Reaper's realm could be beautiful but disconcerting; look, but not too closely, touch, but don't feel.

Her gut turned over, and inside her rounded belly, the baby stirred as if sensing the return of her anxiety.

Except that *anxiety* was too mellow a word for what she was experiencing. Really, she was flat-out terrified, mere moments away from seeing her husband for the first time in months. For the first time since she'd left him.

And he didn't have a clue that she was pregnant.

She almost regretted telling Reaver that she didn't need him to accompany her down here when he'd flashed her from Ares's Greek island to the outer portal. She should have at least allowed Maleficent, a hellhound that had shadowed her everywhere on the island, to come with her. The hound had refused to leave her side until Cara distracted the beast long enough for Lilliana to get away. She was going to miss the moose-sized canine, but Cara assured her that Mal would find her if the hellhound had bonded with her.

Lilliana was going to have a hard enough time trying to explain bringing home a baby, let alone a pet that ate people.

Resting her palm on her baby bump, she stepped off the landing pad and started toward the palace, her heart pounding wildly. Azagoth would have sensed her presence by now.

Before that thought even faded, the skin on the back of her neck tingled, and she stopped in her tracks.

He was here.

He was behind her.

She should turn around and face him. But damn, she wasn't ready for this.

Closing her eyes, she let out a long, ragged breath, and when she spoke, she could only manage a whisper. "Azagoth."

"Look at me, Lilliana."

The sound of Azagoth's voice, commanding but soft, sent a tremor of emotion through her. They'd spoken almost daily via Skype, so she knew he wanted her to come home. But how would he feel about their child after he'd once told her he didn't want any more children? How would he feel about the fact that she'd kept this from him for nine months?

Bracing herself for anything, she swung around.

Dark power emanated from Azagoth as he stood a few feet away, his glossy obsidian wings folded rigidly behind him, his short hair as black as his shoes, slacks, and shirt. He'd rolled up the sleeves, revealing tattoos he'd stolen from Thanatos, and his hands were clenched at his sides.

She couldn't read him at all, and she wasn't sure how to process that.

His emerald eyes met hers for a mere heartbeat and then dropped to her belly.

"I guess I have something to tell you..."

The sound of laughter came from somewhere behind her, and Azagoth's head snapped back up as two of his sons, Journey and Maddox, came into view just up the path. The two Memitim were goofing off with their cell phones, oblivious to the fact that in a moment they were going to be in the middle of something they didn't want to be anywhere near.

Azagoth hissed, his wings unfurling as he swept her into his arms and lifted her into the air. The breath whooshed from her lungs as the ground fell away, but Azagoth tucked her close, his grip secure but gentle even as he dive-bombed his startled sons. He banked hard, forcing them to the ground before shooting across the courtyard to land on the balcony outside their bedroom.

Lilliana swayed a little as she found her footing, but Azagoth's arm remained in place, a solid band of support. "Azagoth—"

"Shh." He covered her mouth with his in a desperate kiss. "I've missed you," he whispered against her lips.

God, she'd missed him too, and with a cry of relief, she melted against him.

* * * *

Azagoth moaned at the taste of Lilliana on his lips. It was as if he'd been starving for months and had finally been given a morsel of gourmet cuisine.

It wasn't enough, was merely an appetizer, and he cursed as he broke the kiss and stepped back to avoid crushing her belly.

Her *pregnant* belly.

Holy shit.

She looked up at him with big amber eyes. "So you aren't angry?"

Fuck, yeah, he was. But no. How could he be? Yes. No. Fuck. There were so many emotions tangled up inside him that he wasn't sure how to answer. Obviously, she'd been pregnant for months and hadn't told him. Had she known she was pregnant when she left him? Who else knew while he'd been kept in the dark like a fool?

Yeah, he was a little steamed. But he was also a jackass who'd pushed her away in the first place.

Screw it. It was too complicated and frankly, he didn't give a shit right now. He had other needs to address, like the fact that Lilliana was home and even his evil side was thrilled.

And it wanted to claim its mate.

"I'll sort it out later," he said roughly as he fisted her skirt and yanked it up. "Right now I need you."

"*Yes.*" She threw herself against him, wrapping her arms around him as she hooked his thigh with her leg. "Hurry."

Her nails dug into his shoulders and her swollen belly pressed into his abs and there was no way this was going to work.

As carefully as his desperation would allow, he spun her around and braced her against the railing.

She looked around at him from over her shoulder, her long chestnut hair draped across her back, her mouth quirked in a naughty smile that hit him right in the cock. "Right here?"

Snarling with impatience, he spared a second to look out at his domain. A group of Unfallen and Memitim were wandering around and glancing up at the balcony while trying not to look obvious. Journey and Maddox must have a fucking loudspeaker.

With a thought and a whisper, a thick black fog rolled in from the outer edges of his realm, shrouding the land in darkness and his balcony in privacy.

"Nice," she murmured.

No, there was nothing nice about it. That fog could have contained acid, poison, or millions of flesh-eating creatures if he'd wished it. As it was, it would leave an ashen residue on everything it touched. He'd have to summon rain later.

Then they could make love in that, too.

She left you. She lied to you.

Yes, she had. But he hadn't been a pillar of virtue either, so he quashed his inner voice, because right now he needed to connect with her, to re-establish their bond...if not their trust.

She seemed to agree, her hand stretching back to grip his thigh and pull him even closer. The heat of her palm though his slacks was nearly his undoing. It had been so long. Too long.

As he reached beneath her skirt and tore away her panties, he swore they'd never be apart like that again. Never.

His fingers found her wet and swollen, so ready for him it made his knees weak.

Lilliana squirmed with anticipation, her slender shoulders rising and falling with every panting breath. Her nails dug into his leg so hard that it was painful. Deliciously, sinfully painful.

"Hurry," she whispered again.

Some part of him wanted to deny her request—the part of him that was angry about being lied to. It wanted to drag this out, to punish her with pleasure.

The logical part of him realized that wasn't much of a punishment.

The horny part of him just couldn't freaking wait.

With a growl, he ripped open his fly.

She moaned as he pressed the head of his erection against her center, but even though he wanted to drive into her with a frenzied thrust, he was careful. His child was inside her, and he wasn't going to risk hurting either one of them.

Very slowly, he eased inside her welcoming heat, her slick walls gripping his shaft in an erotic caress.

He wasn't going to last long, but that was okay. The love of his life had come back to him, and they had eons to make up for lost time.

She sighed his name as he filled her, and the sigh became a husky "Yes" when he began to move, initiating a slow rhythm that was still almost too fast.

"I missed this," he rasped, his grip tightening on her hips.

He pumped into her, his thrusts coming harder and faster as the pleasure spread and intensified. The soft sounds Lilliana made as she pushed against him, meeting every stroke with enthusiasm, drove him even higher. They'd been a perfect sexual match from the beginning, and after almost a year of separation, nothing had changed.

The first stirrings of climax tingled in his balls and the base of his spine, and before he got too carried away, he thrust his hand between her legs and found her swollen bud. She cried out, bucking at the instant orgasm.

Her pleasure triggered his, and he roared in ecstasy that went beyond the physical. It was mental, emotional, so powerful his wings erupted and shrouded them in a cocoon of passion as he emptied himself inside her. His release peaked, ebbed, and peaked again, repeating the cycle over and over until he lost count and his legs would barely support him.

Finally, as his lust eased, another hunger roared into focus. The intensity of it shocked him, and without thinking, he twisted her head and bit into her throat. She moaned as he took a powerful draw, starved for both the connection and the sweet nectar of nourishment only she could give.

Somewhere in the back of his mind he knew he should be more gentle, but before he could tame his inner beast, another voice pierced his awareness.

Father.

The baby. Holy hell, he could *feel* the baby.

He was a father thousands of times over, but he hadn't even met most of his children. Those he did know hadn't come into his life until they were decades, if not centuries, old. This was the first time he'd hold his own infant offspring. The first time he'd fathered a child with a female he loved.

This was *everything* to him.

The fog dispelled and the sky above turned brilliant blue as his world became right again. He tightened his massive wings around their bodies, shielding them from view.

"Azagoth," she gasped. "The sky. It's never been so bright."

Sated and riding a killer dopamine high, he swiped his tongue over the bite wound to seal it and gathered her against him. After nine agonizing months of separation from his mate, hours of bone-crushing loneliness was at an end.

"Lilli," he murmured, as he gently pulled her upright so her back was to his chest and they were still connected. "I love you so much."

She brought one of his hands down to her belly, and his heart fluttered at the movement beneath his palm. "I love you too."

They were going to have to talk after this. Talk a lot.

But right this minute he was going to revel in the gift he'd just been given.

His mate.

His *baby*.

Chapter Eight

His computer.

His *baby*.

As Cipher grabbed his laptop from the pedestal of ice it had been sitting on, he didn't think he'd ever been happier to see anything in his entire life.

"You assholes better have taken care of it." He ran his hand over the smooth protective case. "There's a scratch. See, right there. Fuckers," he muttered.

"Leave us," Lyre said to the demon assholes who'd unlocked the room containing Bael's confiscated loot. "I can handle it from here."

The demons, who looked and smelled like bloated human corpses wrapped in burlap bags, shuffled across the ice floor and fur rugs toward the door. Before this, Cipher had seen very little of Bael's castle, but now it seemed that everything had been constructed of either ice, bones, or fur, and nothing melted...not even the working fireplaces made of ice.

Even the door they'd come through had been constructed of opaque, charcoal-colored ice. According to Lyre, Bael missed the extravagant crystal palaces in Heaven, so he'd created a replica of his former home out of enchanted ice that could withstand the intense heat from the nearby volcano and the moat filled with lava.

Cipher doubted the stronghold was a genuine, exact replica, though, given the scenes of torture carved into the walls by an incredibly talented artist. Everything was so...graphic. Had Bael been a sick, twisted bastard as a fully-haloed angel too?

Cipher waited until the door closed behind the ugly bastards to fire up his baby. When he did, the whirr of the CPU fan damn near made him orgasm.

But it wouldn't have been like the one Lyre gave you.

He nearly groaned out loud at that thought.

Lyre stood nearby, her lush midnight hair tied up in a severe high knot, her mouth little more than a grim slash. She didn't seem nearly as excited to be here as he'd figured she'd be. Bael was going to reward her for this, give her a promotion or some shit. She should be grinning like Flail did when she caused him pain. Instead, ever since Lyre picked him up after he'd showered and dressed, she'd been distracted. Maybe a little sad.

Not that he cared.

When the password screen popped up, he covertly turned the laptop away from Lyre's prying eyes and entered the code. A code that also needed to be entered with *his* fingers, and none other. It was the reason none of Bael's minions had been able to break into it.

They hadn't known about the tech he'd both developed and installed on his computer.

Dumbasses.

"I can't believe you're going to do this." Lyre handed him a flash drive she'd dug out of her side pants pocket.

"I'm tired of living in a deep freeze," he said, and that wasn't a lie.

But mainly...mainly he needed to buy a little freedom. And some goodwill. He wasn't a fool—Lyre and Flail were in a competition to see who could get the list from him first. He wouldn't save Flail if she were being roasted over a Neethul fire pit, but if he helped out Lyre he might get something in return. A favor, or maybe even a measure of trust, which he could exploit when the time came.

If he played his cards right, he could actually escape this hell.

The screen flashed, giving him an option to select one of three private blocks on his hard drive. His gaming partition wasn't protected, but he didn't need that one. He'd password-protected the second partition, but he'd set it up so that if, on the insanely minuscule chance someone got into his computer, they'd eventually be able to get into his basic work files. There was some sensitive shit in there about Azagoth's realm and tech, but nothing so critical that Sheoul-gra would be compromised if it were to get out. There were also some nasty booby traps and a computer virus that would execute once the file was downloaded to another computer.

The third partition required blood to open. Blood and a password spoken only in his voice as he typed it.

"I need you to turn around," he said.

"Why?"

"I want to look at your ass."

She blinked. "Really?"

Yes, but that wasn't the main reason. Also, she was seriously gullible. How had she survived this long in Sheoul?

"Do you want the list or not?"

Rolling her eyes, she spun on her heel and faced the wall. "Oh, and in case you had any ideas about contacting Azagoth or your friends, think again. The ice in this room blocks all electronic signals, including WIFI."

Fuck. There went a major piece of his plan. The *heroes ride in and save the day* part. Guess he was on his own.

Unfortunately, lack of access also meant he couldn't disable Bael's security systems, which would render escape far more difficult, especially since Bael had embraced tech in ways other wretched warlords in Sheoul hadn't. Most still lived in the Dark Ages.

Cursing silently, he nicked his thumb with a fang and smeared a drop of blood on the touchpad. His fingers settled over keys so worn that most of the letters had faded as he whispered, "Han Solo."

Take that, Hawkyn. Star Wars beats Star Trek. Every. Single. Time.

Hawk would probably break his jaw for that, but it would be worth it.

A twinge of regret pricked him. He missed Sheoul-gra. He missed his buddy. Missed all of his friends.

But they were looking for him. He knew they were.

Doubt came roaring in on the heels of that thought. Hawkyn, Maddox, Journey, Emerico...they had been his anchors after his fall from Heaven, but as Hawkyn liked to say—taken from Trek, of course, "The needs of the many outweigh the needs of the few...or the one."

Which meant that if the risk of rescuing him was too great, he'd become a sacrifice for the greater good. It made sense. But that didn't make it suck any less.

"Can I turn around?" Lyre's smoky voice startled him into the present.

"No."

He tapped on the keyboard, the sound of clicking keys as satisfying as a cold beer on a hot day. He even typed out a few unnecessary strokes just so he could hear the sweet music as he brought up the files containing all the research he'd done to find Azagoth's children in the human realm.

The thousands of files on hundreds of kids had been organized into age groups, with the largest collection being the oldest of his Memitim children. The plan had been to bring in the oldest first, allowing them to get the lay of the land and get settled in before bringing in the younger ones who would need more care. Before Cipher was kidnapped and dragged to Sheoul, they'd been in phase one of the operation.

It had been several months since then. The oldest children should have been collected and safely ensconced inside Azagoth's realm by now. He'd give Bael that list, and while the bastard's minions were hunting the children, not knowing they'd already been gathered and taken to Azagoth, he could be plotting an escape.

He punched a few keys, and the list popped up. Forty names, kids in their teens spread out all over the world. Hopefully, all were safe.

Please let them be safe.

He couldn't be responsible for the death of a single one of them.

"What's the matter?"

He started, glancing over at Lyre, who had turned around at some point. "Nothing. Why?"

"You look like you're having second thoughts."

"Second thoughts?" He snorted. "About giving a monster access to the Grim Reaper's innocent children so he can do God knows what with them? No, it's really no problem."

"Innocent? Memitim?" She waved her hand in dismissal. "They're warriors, same as every other angel."

He frowned at her. "You're kidding, right?"

"No." Her long fingers drifted to the blade she always kept at her hip, and he suddenly wondered how good she was with the thing. Was it for show, or could she really dance with danger? "I mean, they aren't full angels with wings, but they do have powerful fighting abilities."

She didn't know. She truly didn't have a clue. "This isn't a list of adult Memitim. It's a list of the little ones still living in the human realm with human parents. They don't even know they're angels, and they don't get their powers until they're adults."

"What?" Her fingers faltered. "I didn't know it was those ones. I thought he wanted Memitim."

"Would it make a difference?"

She gave a haughty sniff as she looked down at her boot. "Of course not."

"Of course not," he muttered. "Do you know what he plans to do with them?"

"No idea." She glanced back up at him. "So what is this list anyway? I mean, obviously it's a list of his children, but why is there a list of them at all? Doesn't Azagoth have thousands of them?"

Many thousands. The dude had been prolific over the eons. "You know how he sired over seventy children a year for thousands of years to create Memitim, right?"

"Of course. That's basic angel knowledge." She gazed up at the ceiling as she recited Azagothic knowledge straight from the history tomes. "His children, born to full angel mothers, are given to human families to raise. They don't learn the truth until adulthood, when they're told the truth about their roots. As their new angelic powers emerge, they're trained to be earthbound guardian angels, working to keep special humans called Primori safe until they eventually earn their wings and ascend to Heaven." A fierce blush spread across her cheeks when she saw him staring at her. "He was one of my favorite historical characters, so he was my focus in my history courses and research."

"Research?"

"It was sort of my job when I was an angel."

Sounded boring as fuck.

"Yeah, well, now that he's mated, he's no longer siring Memitim and wants to bring all children who remain in the human realm to Sheoul-gra." Cipher casually deleted all remaining files related to Azagoth's kids and then ran the virtual shredder program he'd developed. "It took forever for Heaven to agree, but they finally gave him the names and last known locations of those children."

"Hmm." Lyre's pert nose wiggled as she ran the information through her processor. It was cuter than it should be. "Maybe he's going to blackmail Azagoth for something. He's had a bug up his ass about Azagoth ever since I arrived."

Interesting. "And when was that?"

"Not long after the near-apocalypse."

Which was just a few years ago. "That explains it," he murmured as he looked back down at his screen.

"Explains what?"

"Why you don't radiate evil." He deleted more files related to Azagoth and his realm. "You're not completely saturated with it yet."

"I am too," she said, a little defensively. She might as well have stomped her foot, and he gave her a skeptical glance.

"How much time did you spend as an Unfallen?" he asked.

"None."

"None?" Ooh, he should probably delete that porn file. "You were captured and dragged down here right away?"

"No." Her sterling eyes flashed as her defenses came up. This seemed to be a touchy subject for her. He'd have to file that information away. "I came of my own free will."

So she was another Flail. She'd *wanted* to expose herself to the evils of Sheoul. He had absolutely no respect for shitbags like that.

Although he had to admit that she didn't strike him as being anything like Flail. Aside from wanting the list of Azagoth's minor children, anyway. Not that it mattered. He was going to get out of this hellhole and would hopefully never see either of them again.

He jammed the flash drive into the USB port and downloaded the file containing the names that would hopefully buy him some time.

"Done." His gut churned as he unplugged the drive and held it out to Lyre. "Tell Bael to shove it up his ass."

The merest hint of a smile teased her lips. He shouldn't find it sexy, but he did. A lot.

"As much as I'd love to say that, I'll let you tell him yourself." She bounced the little drive in her palm, and her expression grew serious. "Cipher, I hope whatever you put on this drive isn't a trick, because if it is, we'll both pay with blood. And when I recover, I'll show you just how saturated with evil I am."

He doubted the threat would have sounded as cute coming from Flail. But in any case, she didn't have anything to worry about. There were no tricks on the flash drive.

At least, none Bael would find out about until Cipher was long gone.

Chapter Nine

The flash drive felt like victory in Lyre's palm as she walked Cipher toward Bael's throne room. *Take that, Flail. I won. Big time.*

She glanced over at Cipher, whose expression was stony. Unreadable.

But it hadn't been that way when he'd downloaded the list or talked about the names on it.

Names of children.

An unexpected wave of guilt engulfed her. She'd known Bael and Moloc were after Memitim, trained adults who could handle themselves. But the revelation that these were young children left her spinning and struggling to conceal it.

Dammit, it shouldn't bother her. She was a fallen angel. A willing fallen angel. She should be sweating evil from her very pores by now. Evil that would allow her to not care. To maybe even enjoy the suffering of innocents.

Instead, she was slow-walking the damned list and wondering what Bael was going to do with it.

But she couldn't stall forever, and they finally arrived at Bael's residence. Two sleek, black-haired Canis demons, drool dripping from their canine jaws, let them inside.

Bael and his brother Moloc were huddled over a map with Rancor, a female fallen angel who had gained control of the Horun region after a coup backed by the brothers.

All three fallen angels had sworn allegiance to Revenant, but before

Lyre had fallen, she'd uncovered evidence that they were secretly working against him. At the time and as a historian, she'd been fascinated by the political dynamics in Sheoul, even as she was disturbed by the Satan loyalists. The Powers That Be in Heaven didn't openly admit they were backing Revenant as the King of Hell, but he was definitely preferable over the imprisoned alternative.

But as a fallen angel betrayed by her Heavenly family, Lyre had intentionally chosen to sell her services to an enemy of Revenant. Hell, she'd come to Bael within an hour of falling.

She'd regretted it by the next day.

But there was no point in dwelling on the consequences of her rash decision, and as long as she got what she wanted out of the deal, she'd consider her choice well made.

Probably.

The three fallen angels turned as a unit to face her and Cipher.

As she held out the flash drive, Bael grinned, his fangs glistening in air made smoky by the torch sconces. He had access to the best technology demons could devise or steal from humans, but his taste in decor ran medieval drab.

"Finally." He pinned Cipher with an intense stare. "You're ready to serve me."

"Serve *you?*" Cipher laughed, and Lyre cringed. Bael didn't appreciate being mocked. "You don't deserve my loyalty. I'll serve Sheoul's cause, but not yours."

Bael's lip curled, revealing wicked, lion-sized fangs. "Sheoul's cause *is* my cause."

"Then tell me how my list is going to be used." Cipher's deep voice was calm, steady, but his gaze smoldered with hate. "I can't imagine that hurting Azagoth's children is in Sheoul's ultimate best interest."

"That," Bael said, "is none of your concern." He fingered the drive. "If this is a trick, I'll kill you."

"Fuck you," Cipher growled, and this time Lyre nodded in approval. Bael might not like being mocked, but he respected good, old-fashioned aggression. "Those are the names of all Azagoth's children who remain in the human realm."

Bael tossed the drive to his brother Moloc, who plugged it into a tablet on a nearby table. After a moment, Moloc looked over. "There are only forty names here. How can there be so few?"

"Most of the children have already been gathered and taken to

Sheoul-gra."

"If you're lying—"

"Yeah, yeah." Cipher tucked his hands in his jeans pockets, all casual, as if he wasn't standing in a nest of vipers. "You'll kill me."

Moloc's dark eyes went as black as a poisonous Sheoulin rose. Of the two brothers, he was the calmest, the one least prone to irrational actions. But he was also the smartest, which made him far more terrifying than Bael.

"Killing you will only be the beginning," he said as he shoved the tablet aside.

Rancor eyed Cipher the way Lyre eyed a juicy burger, and the creepy eyeballs dangling from her bracelet and necklace matched her hungry stare.

"What do you plan to do with him now?" Rancor licked her lips, and Lyre bristled. "Come work for *me*, and I'll treat you well."

"He's mine," Bael snapped. "I risked a lot to steal him from Azagoth."

"I belong to no one." Cipher looked each of the three fallen angels in the eye, and Lyre had to give him points for bravery. Or stupidity. Time would tell, she supposed. "I've given you what you want. Now give me what you promised. My freedom."

Bael reached for his favorite cup made from the skull of an angel. Looked like it was full of blood. "Until you've proven your loyalty, your freedom will be limited."

The anger smoldering in Cipher's eyes sparked blue fire. His growing ire shouldn't be sexy, but it was. It was that same intense but quiet fury that she'd found attractive in Dailon before he went vigilante on someone.

"That wasn't the deal, Bael."

"You didn't come to us willingly," Moloc said, sounding all reasonable and calm. "You have to earn your freedom."

Bael lowered the cup from his mouth and licked blood from his lips. "Worry not, worm, I'll find a use for you. One befitting your cyberskills."

"Yes," Rancor purred. "With your fallen angel powers, you could wreak havoc through the demonweb and human internet, and the viruses you could create, ones that can infect living creatures...yes, you'll be invaluable."

For a moment, Lyre thought Cipher would balk, but then he

shrugged. "Sounds fun."

Bael watched Cipher over the rim of his cup as he drank, and when he lowered the vessel from his mouth, blood dripped from his lips. "I'll give you more freedom, only with Lyre by your side. Betray my goodwill, and I'll eat your intestines for breakfast." He flicked his wrist. "Begone, worm. Lyre, stay."

Lyre bowed her head in acknowledgement and said to Cipher under her breath, "Wait outside for me. Go. Before he changes his mind." Bael was likely to do breakfast now if Cipher didn't get the hell out of there.

With one last glare at everyone, including her, Cipher left. And she might have watched his retreating backside a little longer than appropriate before turning back to the three regional bosses.

"I did what you asked," she said. "What Flail failed to do. I want to talk about how I'm going to get my revenge."

"This again?" Bael curled his lip in contempt. "I have more important things to do."

"Like what?" Disappointment made her words curt, but dammit, she was tired of waiting. "What are you using those names for?"

Rancor looked up from poking one of the blinking eyeballs on her bracelet. "It's all part of the plan to release Satan from his prison."

Release Satan from prison? She'd heard talk of it, but as far as she knew, no one truly believed such a thing was possible.

"How can that be?" she demanded. "According to prophecy, he's got nearly a thousand years to go before he's released."

"Prophecy." Moloc scoffed, waving his claw-tipped hand. "There are endless interpretations of every prophecy. Even if we must wait until then, we will need all of the souls in Sheoul-gra on our side for the Final Battle between Heaven and Hell."

"Bullshit!" Bael threw his cup across the room, splashing blood all over the ice wall and freezing it instantly. "We will not wait! Azagoth will release the souls, and he'll—"

Moloc's hand came down on Bael's shoulder, easing his frenzy within seconds. Bael was prone to sudden angry fits and, somehow, his brother could always bring him down with something as minor as a touch.

"You should go," Moloc told her.

Only a fool would stay after being told to leave.

Apparently, Lyre was a fool. "Not until Bael tells me how he plans to help me get revenge on those who wronged me."

"Patience, female," Moloc said. "The war between Heaven and Hell will draw out the angels you seek to destroy."

Wait...*that* was the plan? Do nothing? She could have done that herself. "That's nothing but a byproduct of a war destined to happen! I don't want to wait a thousand years!"

"Neither do I," Moloc murmured. "Neither do I."

"Go, my love." Bael broke away from his brother. "Unbind Cipher's wings and let him discover his fallen angel talents. We will have use for them soon enough."

Bastards. All of this for nothing. Well, not nothing. She'd outmaneuvered Flail and gained some points with Moloc and Bael.

But still, none of this felt like a win.

Chapter Ten

Lyre had emerged from Bael's residence with one hell of a scowl on her gorgeous face. She'd said only that she was going to unbind his wings, and then she'd been silent as they hurried out of the massive ice castle. Once outside on the drawbridge that spanned a lava moat, she flashed them both to a bizarre land of gray desert sand, craggy hills, and weird, scrawny vegetation.

"Where are we?" He sidestepped to avoid a spiky black vine slithering toward his crude leather boots.

A prison guard had thrown the blister-spawning footwear at him, along with a pair of seriously beat-up jeans and a T-shirt that must have belonged to some other prisoner, on the way to the shower. Which was really just a drain in the slaughterhouse and a bucket of tepid water. Damn, he hated Sheoul.

"We're in the middle of nowhere."

"I can see that." Another vine, this one red and pulsing like a vein, followed them for a few steps. "I thought you were going to unbind my wings."

"I am. Somewhere safe." She led him toward a flat expanse of sand and gravel, her expression still creased with whatever disappointment Bael and his cohorts had dished out. "Your powers and wings didn't develop the way they should have, over the course of months or years. So when your wings pop out, who knows what's going to happen? Besides, we don't even know *why* your wings developed practically overnight."

Yeah, he'd love an answer as to why he'd woken up with the wing anchors on his back sewn shut, his wings bound inside, the day after being abducted. The official story, that they'd emerged while he was unconscious and that a sorcerer had been immediately called to bind them, seemed fishy to him. No one grew wings that fast, and binding them before knowing what powers they brought with them struck him as short-sighted.

Then again, Bael didn't always operate on logic or with forethought. Impulsive, narcissistic, and emotional, Bael was a dictator whose personal whims took him on wild boondoggles. If not for Moloc's restraining presence, Cipher doubted the guy could preside over his own bowel movements, let alone an entire territory.

"So you brought me to this wasteland so I wouldn't destroy anything."

"Exactly." She stopped in the center of the clearing, and all around them, the vegetation quivered as if excited by their presence. "Take off your shirt and turn around."

He'd say something blatantly inappropriate if he weren't vibrating out of his skin in anticipation of feeling his wings explode from his back. Of feeling power flood him once more. Yes, it was going to be dark energy, but after going without that unique ecstasy for so long, he was eager to experience any kind of power again.

Would it be different than the sensation of letting in Heavenly power? Would it be as addictive?

Lyre slid the blade from the sheath at her hip. "Are you ready?"

He opened his mouth to say yes, but his anticipation suddenly mixed with doubt. This would be the first step toward acceptance of his new life as a fallen angel. There would be no going back once he opened the floodgates to the evil that surrounded him.

But what choice did he have? Without the wings, he was powerless here, and he needed every advantage he could get to escape Bael's clutches.

"Cipher?" Lyre's hand came down lightly on the small of his back, and he jerked out of his thoughts.

"Yeah," he said roughly. He needed to do this, but he swore he'd do whatever it took to keep evil from consuming him completely. "But what's to keep me from flashing out of Bael's territory and escaping?"

"The same thing that happens to all Unfallen brought here against their will." Pity turned the silver in her eyes liquid, like a spoon full of water, and he knew he wasn't going to like whatever she had to say. "Bael had an Orphmage curse your wings with a tethering spell. You can't leave his realm until he trusts you and the curse is lifted."

Well, shit. That trashed his immediate plans for escape. But he wasn't going to give up. If he could get a message to Hawkyn, he could warn him about the list Cipher had given to Bael, and his friends could find a way to get him out of here.

He peeled off his T-shirt and bared his back to Lyre. "Do it."

He felt a whisper of air as Lyre brought the knife up to the twin scars near his shoulder blades, the wing anchors from which his new flappers would emerge. The blade's cold tip sliced into his skin, and he gritted his teeth against the pain. Lyre made two cuts and worked quickly, severing the binding twine that had kept his wings imprisoned.

"Done."

She hadn't needed to tell him that.

Every cell in his body sang with power, as if he'd just been plugged in to Sheoul's main battery. Pleasure-pain tore through his back and shoulders as pale gray, bat-like wings erupted in a violent spray of blood-red gelatinous membrane.

Nasty.

That was *not* how his lemon-tipped white Heavenly wings had popped out the first time.

He didn't have a chance to ponder more. An ice cold stream of energy shot down his arm and blasted from his fingertips, launching him backward in a tumble of dust and flapping, leathery wings.

"What the fuck?"

"Oh, wow!" Sheathing her dagger, Lyre jogged toward him. "That was dissolving ice. Look."

A column of ice had encased one of the tentacle shrubs, freezing it solid. But as they watched, it melted rapidly, turning the plant to liquid as it went. Within moments, there was nothing but a puddle where the shrub had been.

The other shrubs were frozen too, but not in ice. In fear.

That was pretty badass.

"I told you this could be chaotic—"

He threw out a hand to warn Lyre off. His control sucked, which he proved as a fireball shot at her from the palm of his hand.

Fire engulfed her, demon-faced flames that laughed and bit at her. No! Oh, shit. He felt her screams all the way to his gut as she fell to the ground and writhed in violent agony.

"*Soretay*! Stop!" He yelled commands in Sheoulic as he rushed toward her, but his words were useless.

He dove on top of her, covering her with his body. He tried to wrap his ugly-ass wings around her, but the fuckers didn't behave, instead fanning the flames, beating the both of them as they flapped uselessly.

Then, for no reason he could figure out, the shrieking apparitions flickered out. Lyre went limp beneath him, her exhausted, panting breaths puffing hot air against his neck.

"Wow," she rasped. "That was unexpected."

He pushed himself up on one arm and looked down at her. Scorch marks streaked her face and her clothes were singed. The hemline of her shirt was completely gone, leaving her flat belly exposed, a smudge of soot forming a crescent under her navel.

He wanted to clean it off with his tongue. Too bad she was playing for the wrong team.

You're playing for the same team now.

No, he wasn't. He might be a fallen angel, but not by choice. And, until evil took him over completely, he wasn't in league with them yet. And he'd never play for Bael the Seriously Unstable. Right now he had no choice, but once he figured out these new powers, he was going to get the fuck out of here.

"You can let me up anytime now," Lyre said softly. "Preferably before one of your new powers incinerates or melts me."

"Right." He jumped up and offered her a hand.

"Thanks, but no." Eyeing his hand like it was a viper, she pushed to her feet and backed away from him. "I'm just going to watch from...over there." She pointed to a bluff in the distance. The far distance.

It was probably for the best. With little to lose, he was going to test his limits and push his boundaries.

And boundaries? Well, those were something he'd never believed in, and for once, that little personality flaw was going to work for him instead of against him.

Chapter Eleven

Lyre watched Cipher try to get his powers and wings under control for just over twenty-four human hours.

It hadn't gone well. His wings, grotesquely veined with serrated claws at the tips, seemed to have minds of their own. His fallen angel gifts were powerful but unpredictable, like natural disasters spawned by a child's imagination.

Finally, after he exploded a tree with a superheated stream of blue light and nearly fried himself with the blowback, she called down to him.

"You hungry?" she yelled. "Because I could eat."

He let out a frustrated shout accompanied by a stomp of his foot, and a crack appeared in the ground under the sole of his boot. A deafening boom and a slow rumble started up, and within seconds the crack lengthened and began to widen as the walls collapsed and chunks of earth tumbled into the fissure.

That couldn't be good.

"Run!" she shouted.

He sprinted toward her, away from the growing gap. And then, suddenly, he spun around and ran toward it.

"Cipher! No!" What the fuck was he doing?

She extended her wings, ready to go after him as he leaped across the fissure. He wasn't going to make it to the other side of the sheer cliff face. Not if his wings wouldn't work—

His great wings flapped, lifting him easily skyward. He banked and soared in a glorious, elegant arc. A shout of pure joy rang out as he flew toward her, reminding her of the excitement she'd felt the first time she'd tried out her fallen angel wings. Hers had taken a year to grow, but it had taken only minutes to get them working. Cipher had to be thrilled to finally have his under control.

Folding her own black leather wings against her shoulders, she watched him come in for a landing, but as he did, one wing went rogue, freezing in a closed position. He clipped a tree and went into an unrecoverable spin before hitting the ground and tumbling to a stop next to her.

She coughed at the resulting cloud of dust. "That was graceful."

He eyed her from where he lay sprawled in the dirt. "Tell me you got that on video."

She didn't want to be charmed, but she laughed anyway. Humor was something she missed since entering Sheoul. No one had a sense of humor here. And those who did seemed to have found it puddled on the floor of a torture chamber.

"No such luck," she said.

"S'okay. But I'll bet it would have gone viral." Wincing, he shoved to his feet and tried to push his left wing into the retraction position. "I don't get it. I can't control these things. It's like they're fighting me. They don't feel right."

They didn't look right, either. Marred by what seemed to be scars and ragged edges, they weren't like any newbie wings she'd ever seen.

"Hmm. Maybe they were damaged by the restraints." She moved around behind him, silently admiring his broad, muscular back. It would look even better with scratch marks from her fingernails after a long, sweaty round of sex.

She blinked, surprised by her runaway thought. Yes, she'd been prepared to get down and dirty with him in his cell, but that had been nothing but a way to get the list of names from him. A means to an end.

Mostly. It wouldn't have been a hardship, anyway.

But things were different now. She didn't need anything from him, and while he was still a ward of Bael's realm he wasn't exactly a prisoner anymore. And now that his wings were unbound, the strength and power emanating from him wrapped around her like an aphrodisiac.

Didn't hurt that he was gorgeous, either.

Carefully, she nudged his right wing down so she could inspect it, running her palm over the long, flexible bones and thick, rugged expanses.

"How does that feel?"

"I can't feel anything." He looked over his shoulder at her, one lock of blond hair falling across his forehead and giving him a sexy, playful expression. "Are you touching me?"

Not in the way I'd like to be.

Nodding, she flexed one of the joints. "You can't feel this?"

"Not at all."

"Okay, try extending your wing."

Nothing happened. He let out a frustrated curse, and then, finally, the wing shot out before folding in again.

"It shouldn't have taken that much effort, should it? Is this normal?"

"I don't think so."

"You don't *think* so? You're a fallen angel, right?"

She jammed her fists on her hips. "No one is going to want to have sex with you if you're snarky with them, you know."

"*What?*"

Ignoring him, she stretched out one of his wings. "I told you, I've only been a fallen angel for a few years. It's not like I know everything about every fallen angel's experience." She poked at a blemish in a large expanse of the tough, leathery membrane. "But from what I've heard, once the wings erupt for the first time, it only takes a couple of hours to figure out the basics. You should have been flying hours ago." She dragged her finger down the long bone toward the base, her finger tingling from the electric sizzle emanating from it. "Were they sensitive at first?"

"Not at all. Should they have been?"

That was one thing everyone, including herself, remembered about their new wings. Sensitivity to the point of agony at the lightest touch. After the sensitivity eased, wings became erogenous zones. Cipher should be practically groaning in pleasure right now. Hell, she was nearly there and they weren't even her wings.

"Mine were crazy sensitive," she murmured as she zeroed in on a scar that circled the base of the wing, right where it emerged from the skin. She palpated it, feeling for deformities. "Does that hurt?"

"No. Why?"

"It's a scar. Like a ligature mark, maybe. Must be where the twine was wrapped." She checked the other wing and found a twin scar. Yikes. Her own wings throbbed in sympathy. He must have been in so much pain when his wings were bound. "Same thing on the other one."

"Makes sense." He rolled his broad shoulders, and she nearly drooled. "My wings aren't sensitive now, but they hurt like hell until you took the rope off."

Once, while researching the great demonic war of 263 BC, she'd interviewed a fallen angel whose wings had been bound after capture by an enemy. He'd said the pain was so great he'd taken a sword to his own back in an effort to cut the twine. Would Cipher have done the same if he'd had access to a weapon?

She shuddered. "I'm sorry they did this to you."

"Are you?" he asked as he turned to face her.

"Why would I lie?"

He looked at her like she was an idiot. "Because you're a fallen angel."

"I hate to point out the obvious," she said, "but so are you. And who did you trust before? You were Unfallen, living with the Grim Reaper and his unholy *griminions* and fallen servants. Did you trust them?"

"Some of them," he said, going on the defensive. "A lot of them are Memitim. Memitim who are working toward becoming full-fledged Heavenly angels."

She shook her head, knowing exactly how *un*-trustworthy angels were, fully-haloed or not, *family* or not. "If you trust any angel, you're a fool."

"I trust my friends." His big wings flapped in irritation, and a lightning bolt shot from one of them. The bolt vaporized a nearby cactus, and he gave her a sheepish smile. "Oops."

His wings folded and obediently disappeared.

"So where are they now, these friends? Do you think they're searching for you?" She raked him critically with her gaze, from his muscular legs and hard-cut upper torso to his square, masculine jaw and intelligent eyes. She appreciated all of that, but his friends would see him very differently. "What do you think they'd do if you showed up looking like this? Fallen angel wings and a dark soul? They'll turn on you. They'll kill you, Cipher."

"No, they won't."

She'd had faith in her own friends and family once too. And, like Cipher, she hadn't listened to warnings. "Like I said, you're a fool."

"Sounds like someone is a little bitter." One blond eyebrow went up in a quizzical arch. "Betrayed by friends, I'm guessing?"

"Family." She looked out over the scorched and cratered field of destruction Cipher had wrought upon the earth and vegetation. "But friends abandoned me too. It was fun. Lots of fun."

At least none of her family had *enjoyed* watching as she was held down and her wings severed. They'd been devastated. Her sisters, even the one who had betrayed her, had cried. Her mother, wracked by sobs, had collapsed in grief. And her father, ever stoic and suffering from a perpetual stiff upper lip, had managed to scrounge up a tear to shed.

Although she couldn't be sure if the tear was for her or for his reputation.

How could you, he'd whispered just loudly enough for her to hear as guards escorted her to the chopping block. She'd brought so much shame and dishonor down on her family, and all for a male.

But that male had been worth the risk. If not for her own poor judgment in confiding in her sister, no one would have found out that she'd fallen for a demon.

She'd played that day over and over in her head, wishing she'd never told Lihandra about him, and she definitely regretted arranging for them to meet. If only Lihandra could have seen the good in him, a champion for those who couldn't get justice any other way. For those who couldn't stand up for themselves.

And now he was dead, Lyre was disgraced, and her sister got to justify what she'd done by saying she'd done it for Lyre's own good and that she hadn't meant for Lyre to lose her wings.

Right.

As an angel named Lyresiel, Lyre had a contentious relationship with her older sister. She and Lihandra had never agreed on anything, had gone almost a century without speaking once, and had driven her parents and younger sister, Bellagias, mad with their fighting. But Lyre had never believed Lihandra hated her so much that she'd turn Lyre in for "copulating with a demon."

Lyre hadn't "copulated" with anyone, but that hardly mattered to the angelic council that presided over such matters. That she *would* have copulated with said demon was what mattered. Oh, yes, she'd admitted all the things she'd wanted to do with him.

I'd have let him take my virginity, and then I'd have ridden him until we both passed out. And then we'd have done it in our dreams, because he had the power to connect us that way, too.

Every member of the council had gone apoplectic. But her erotic agenda wasn't what had gotten her kicked out of Heaven. Nope. They'd been willing to cut her some slack and write her dalliance off as a youthful transgression. Oh, there would have been some severe punishment, of course, but compared to losing one's wings, it would have been a slap on the wrist.

No, she'd have gotten off easy.

If they just hadn't gone and killed her demon.

* * * *

So Lyre had been betrayed by her family.

That had to suck.

Cipher, for all his faults, had been lucky enough to have a supportive family. Sure, when he'd fucked up and lost his wings they'd been disappointed, but neither his parents nor any of his twenty-two siblings had trashed him. A couple had even reached out to him during his time in Sheoul-gra, keeping in contact and relaying messages from his parents.

But that was before. When he'd been an Unfallen trying to earn his way back into Heaven. How would they react to his becoming a True Fallen? Was Lyre right? Would his friends and family turn on him? Try to kill him?

Lyre seemed lost in thought, her gaze going somewhere he couldn't go. The weird thing was that he wanted to. Because as much as he figured he should hate her, he didn't.

Maybe he just didn't know her well enough to hate her.

Dammit, he wished he had access to the internet or demonweb. He'd love to do a little cyberstalking to find out more about her.

Guess he had to stick with the old-fashioned way. Ugh. Digging up dirt online was so much easier and less talky.

"So," he said, taking the plunge. "How did you lose your wings?"

She jammed her fists on her hips, just above where her low-slung waistband sat. She'd flashed away at some point while he'd been practicing his new powers, and she'd come back with clean clothes free of scorch marks. He definitely approved of the outfit. In the months he'd known her, she'd always worn earth or muted tones, but today's black cargo pants had been paired with a purple tank top that emphasized her perfect, rounded breasts and slender waist. And her combat boots had matching purple laces.

He wondered what color her bra and panties were.

"You know that asking someone how they fell from grace is considered a rude question," she huffed.

Yeah, he had totally sick social skills. "Do I look like I'm concerned about being rude?" He looked down at his palm and summoned a ball of crimson light in an attempt to use his new powers without his wings extended. Maybe he'd have more control this way. One thing that didn't change was the oily, malevolent vibe that skated over the surface of his skin when he was using one of his fallen angel powers. "You don't have to answer if you don't want to."

"No, it's okay," she sighed. "I fell in love with a demon."

"A demon?" His hand jerked in surprise and his ball of light fell to the ground, exploding into a thousand shards of light on impact. "Was he hot? Like, not all scaly and snouty?"

"Of course he was hot," she said as she leaped backward to avoid a spark of super-heated light. "He was a...what are they called? *Ter-taceo*? He looked like any other human male model."

"He was a model?"

"He was a psychotherapist."

Sounded boring as shit. Lots of talky. And he'd bet the guy wasn't even that attractive. "What species?"

"Somniatus."

He revised his thought. *Not* so boring. "A nightmare devil."

Demon slayers claimed they were one of the most dangerous demons there were, attacking their victims in their dreams where they were vulnerable.

She smiled wistfully, and Cipher cursed the trickle of jealousy making its way through his body. He had no reason to be envious of a freaking demon.

Had it fed on her like Cipher had? Had it tasted the sweet nectar that had flowed over his fangs and tongue? The very idea that the guy might have taken her like that made him a little prickly. Again, for no freaking reason.

"He was a nightmare," she said softly, "but only to those who deserved it."

"So he was a benevolent demon? Really?" Color him skeptical. "Somniati feed off of terror."

Her smile turned wicked, matching the gleam in her eyes. "And who better to terrorize than those who hurt others?"

Okay, yeah, he'd give her that. There was no sport in hurting innocents. Bringing a tough-guy asshole to his knees, though...*that* was satisfying.

"So you lost your wings for fucking a demon?" Cipher regretted asking the moment it was out of his mouth, because now he couldn't stop picturing her naked. With another male. "I thought Heaven stopped doing that a few centuries ago."

"They seem to pick and choose," she muttered. "But no, that's not why I got a one-way ticket out of Heaven." She looked off into the distance again, beyond the lake bubbling with shit-brown liquid and the mountain range shaped like skulls, but this time, her expression was etched in anger. "I was to be confined to the Heavenly realm as punishment, so before the sentence was carried out, I went to say goodbye to him. But while I was at his place, we were attacked."

"The Aegis?"

"I *wish* those demon-slaying idiots were the ones who attacked us. They were angels. I fought back. I had to protect him, you know?" She didn't wait for his acknowledgment. "I accidentally killed a novice battle angel who was there to assist in Dailon's capture."

Oh, fuck. "Yeah, that would do it." He made another light ball, but smaller this time. "So they booted you after that?"

"Oh, no," she said, her voice dripping with bitterness. "That would have been too easy. First they forced me to watch as he was tortured and killed."

He winced, having witnessed a few executions by angels making a point. "That had to have sucked."

A few strands of silky hair had escaped her messy bun, and a hot breeze spun up, whipping them around her cheeks, softening her expression. She didn't belong in this hellscape, and for the first time, he wanted to know about her background not for tactical reasons, but for personal ones.

"I knew going into our relationship that we didn't have a shot at a meaningful future, but I wanted time to figure that out, you know?" She cocked her head, watching him with curiosity. "You seem pretty chill about this. You're the most laid-back fallen angel I've ever met."

"Well, I *have* only been fallen for a few years. True Fallen for a few months. You know, since the day I was dragged down here and imprisoned in Bael's ice jail."

A shamed blush bloomed in her cheeks, surprising the shit out of him. "I remember when Bael sent Flail on a mission to infiltrate Azagoth's realm. I was jealous for a while." She gave a bitter laugh. "As a historian, I was dying to meet him."

He frowned as the implications of what she was saying took a dark turn. "So Flail wasn't sent to nab me?"

"Not at first. Bael wanted intel on Azagoth. You just happened to be the best way to get it."

Well, fuck. If he hadn't invited Flail into his bed and, therefore, his life, she'd never have known how important his cyber skills had been to Azagoth. This was all his fault.

Which didn't change the fact that Flail needed to die.

Lyre studied him for a moment, her expression thoughtful. "I'm curious. What were you like as an angel?"

Ah, those were the days. He'd spent them surfing on the Beaches of Paradise, skiing in the Infinite Mountains, and feasting on dishes crafted from decadent ingredients available only in Heaven.

"I was a laid-back son-of-a-bitch," he said. "Pissed off all the Type-As, you know?"

"Is that why you fell?" She tucked a strand of hair behind her ear, and he suddenly wondered if they were sensitive to being nibbled. "Pissed off the wrong asshole?"

"Nah. I slept with a Primori."

"Oh...shit." She stared. "Human?"

"Human virgin whose virginity was the reason she was Primori." His actions had also screwed over Hawkyn, who had been her guardian. He hadn't known Hawkyn at the time, so he hadn't really cared. To this day he couldn't believe Hawk had forgiven him.

"Did you know she was Primori when you slept with her?"

"Yeah."

She stared harder. "Did you know what a Primori was? Like, that they're guarded by Memitim because something about them is important to the fate of the world?"

"Well, I didn't know her virginity was the thing that made her a Primori. And I didn't know she was a virgin until afterward." Still, it was forbidden for any angel to sleep with a human, let alone a human under the protection of Memitim. "But yeah."

"Damn. You're an asshole."

He snorted, because hello, that was obvious. "Yeah."

But if he could take it back, he would. He'd met the human, Felicia, in Fiji, where she was on her honeymoon. Alone. Her fiancé had left her at the altar, and since the honeymoon was paid for, she'd gone alone. She'd been angry and hurt and ready for a vengeful wild fling to give someone else what she'd saved for the man who'd left her.

He'd been at the resort keeping tabs on a demon plotting a cyber attack on several countries, and Felicia had set her sights on him. Being young, arrogant, and really, really easy, he'd been all about hooking up with the hot, tight-bodied woman looking for a way to forget her jackass of a fiancé.

Then Hawkyn had showed up, all, "*Hey, she's Primori, and you need to back the fuck off, Halo.*"

No one told Cipher to back the fuck off.

So he'd ignored the Memitim, and when Hawkyn showed up again, knocking on Felicia's hotel room door just as they were starting to get down and dirty, Cipher had enough. As a full angel, he'd been far more powerful than Hawkyn, and he'd put the Memitim into a temporary coma and flashed him to a deserted island.

Then he'd given Felicia a night to remember.

He had a lot of regrets about that day, but taking care of Felicia wasn't one of them. He shouldn't have had sex with her; that much was clear. But he didn't regret everything else he'd done to help her get through the pain of being betrayed by her fiancé. It wasn't much, but when she'd cried afterward, he'd held her. He'd brought her food and nursed her through a hangover. And when she'd talked about hurting herself, he'd talked her off the ledge.

The day she'd flown back home, he'd been summoned to Heaven for a quick judgment and a wingectomy.

No, sleeping with Felicia hadn't been worth it. He didn't know what her destiny would have been if he hadn't, but just a year ago he'd checked up on her and found that she was a happily married Connecticut dietician with two grown children, grandchildren, and a beach house in Florida. Hopefully, at least for her, her life was better than it would have been if Cipher hadn't interfered.

"Well, come on, asshole," Lyre said, mercifully pulling him out of his past. "We have things to do."

"Food?" he asked hopefully. His stomach was starting to rebel.

"Right after I show you your new home."

He shouldn't be excited about getting a residence in Sheoul, but anything had to be better than where he'd spent the last seven months. "You mean I don't have to sleep on a slab of ice in a prison cell anymore?"

"Nope. If you were a demon, you'd get a filthy hut in some shanty town somewhere. But lucky you, you're a fallen angel, so you get an upgrade." She waggled her dark brows. "In Sheoul, fallen angels are the elite. Like the super-rich in the human world. Different rules apply. Like how you were in the luxury prison."

That had been luxury? He didn't even want to know how much worse it could have been.

"Where do you live?" he asked.

Her wings, midnight black with elegant arches, erupted from her back. "Give me your hand and I'll show you."

He took her hand, liking the way they fit together. "We're going to fly?"

"The curse on your wings prevents you from flashing, even within Bael's realm, so you might as well get used to flying."

He gestured to the dents in the ground where he'd hit it hard. "You saw how well that went."

"That's why I'm holding your hand," she explained. "I'm going to help you."

He didn't have the chance to process his surprise that she was going to take the time to help him get his flying shit together before she'd lifted off, yanking him into the air with her. But he did give a silent thanks, because the quicker he became proficient at this fallen angel stuff, the faster he was going to get out of here.

Maybe she'll come with you.

Startled by that sudden thought, he faltered in flight and nearly took a dive. But Lyre's capable, strong arms caught him, and her wings buoyed them into the endless sky with effortless grace.

Yeah. Maybe she'd come with him.

Or maybe he'd have to kill her.

But it was definitely a predicament for later.

Chapter Twelve

The flight to Lyre's place took twice as long as it should have, but it certainly had been interesting. And sometimes terrifying. Like a test flight of an airplane built by someone who had never seen one.

Cipher definitely failed at Fallen Angel Flying 101, but Lyre gave him an Λ for effort and an A+ for cursing.

"Mother...*fuck!*" He shouted as one wing crumpled and he rolled hard. Lyre barely caught him before he spun out of control and nailed one of the housing structures they were trying to avoid as they flew toward her apartment. "This is bullshit!"

"We're almost there." Clinging to his arm, she guided him between two fifty-story statues of Satan in his ugly beast form. She shuddered, as always, as the statues' eyes followed them. "Bank right."

"Are these apartment buildings?" He flapped his wings hard, but he could barely stay aloft. "They look like giant termite hills turned into beehives."

She'd always thought so too. "Right there." She guided him through an opening near the top of one of the structures and landed on the baked clay floor.

Cipher set down surprisingly gracefully and put away his wings as he looked around. "Nice place."

"I guess." She kicked off her boots. She'd always preferred to go barefoot at home, even if she was only there for a minute. "It's no Heaven."

No, the dwelling was an insult, and not entirely because, as a weakling and a newbie fallen angel, she'd been assigned the tiniest quarters available. It was also just a flat-out affront to the senses. Her house in Heaven had been sprawling and colorful, nestled in a private cloud that floated over a vast, turquoise sea. This...this was small and boring, but she didn't have the motivation to decorate beyond the plush Persian rug in the middle of the room.

Decorating would signify some kind of permanence, and for some reason she didn't want to give in to that kind of thinking, even though she'd basically sold her soul to Bael.

"It's kind of like the dorms in Sheoul-gra." He glanced over at the dining table with seats for two that had never been used. "Except you have a kitchen area."

"Where did you get your meals?"

His sensuous lips curved into wistful smile. "Cafeterias. But the food was good." He noticed that she'd taken off her boots, and he did the same. The polite gesture both amused her and left her off balance. No one in Sheoul was polite. Ever. "It wasn't always that way, though. When I first got to Sheoul-gra, it was a wreck. It was like living in a Tim Burton movie. The Nightmare Before Lilliana."

"The what?"

He chuckled and took in the demon version of cave paintings on the walls that she'd cover up if she wasn't worried about awakening some ancient curse or something. "Life before Azagoth met his mate was way different than the way it is now. Lilliana's awesome."

The sad note in his voice knocked a few bricks out of the wall she was trying really hard to build around her heart. Evil wasn't doing it nearly as quickly as she'd like.

"You really miss Sheoul, don't you?"

"Yeah."

Another brick took a tumble, and that was enough of that. Time to shift gears and subjects.

"Well, I can't do anything about that," she said, "but I can get you your own place. Since I'm still in charge of you, you'll take the apartment next door. Bael had it warded so you can enter but you can't leave through the main entrance." She gestured to the narrow door at the back of her place. "You have to use the doorway connected to mine."

"Are all of these hive-holes connected?"

"Yep." She padded past the bed and headed toward the icebox in the kitchen. She could get a real fridge, but unlike most of the other apartments, hers didn't have electricity.

"How do you keep other people out?" Cipher's footsteps followed behind her. "Wards, I'm guessing?"

"You guessed right. Are you hungry?" Bending over, she opened the little icebox and pulled out a couple of *bludbeouf* wraps she'd picked up yesterday at one of the local markets. "These are kind of like human gyros, except they're made with demon cows. And maybe a little hellrat—"

She broke off when she straightened and caught Cipher staring at her ass. And he didn't even have the decency to pretend that wasn't what he was doing. Instead, he gave her a cocky grin that made heat spread through her pelvis and suspicion spread through her brain.

"What?" he asked, all innocence and charm. "You asked if I was hungry."

She handed him the sandwich and tossed hers to the table. "I'm not buying it."

"What? That you have a fine ass?"

"I'm not buying...this." She gestured to all of him, down to his bare feet. "You're being too nice. Bael had you tortured for months. He forced you to betray your friends and ex-boss, and now you're standing in my apartment with a hard-on and a bad boy smirk? Do you really expect me to believe you're just falling in line like a good little minion of Satan?"

"Revenant," he said as he unwrapped his food.

"What?"

"Revenant is king now." He poked at a dripping shaving of meat hanging from one end of his wrap. "You should have said minion of Revenant."

Not if Bael and Moloc have their way.

"Whatever. What's your game, Cipher?"

Suddenly, her spine was kissing the wall and Cipher was kissing her neck, and where the hell was his sandwich?

"My game," he growled against her throat, "is called Stay Alive. And that means feeling alive. It means taking pleasure where you can so you can survive the shit when it hits. And after seven months of shit, I have one hell of a pleasure deficit."

He was lying. Oh, as his hands tugged her close and his lips sucked at the tender skin at the crook of her shoulder, she knew he was being honest about what he'd said. But he wasn't telling the *entire* truth.

He was distracting her from the truth. He was biding his time until he could either earn his freedom, make his escape, or get revenge before the evil of Sheoul took the choice from him.

And the thing was, she didn't care, because he was right. She needed to feel alive. Needed to fuel up on pleasure, because the bad down here was *really* bad.

Lifting her leg, she hooked it around his thigh. The hard bulge behind his fly rocked against her center as he undulated slowly, a masculine body wave that drove a tingle of excitement from her scalp to her toes. Damn, he was good at this. They hadn't even started and every feminine instinct she had was on board and demanding more.

Cipher lifted his head, a flush staining his cheeks, a primitive hunger in his eyes. She knew how that felt, because she was starving too.

"You okay with this?" His mouth quirked in a teasing smile. "Or do you wanna eat first?"

Was he kidding? "You want to eat?"

"Food? No." He dropped to his knees and in three smooth, fast moves, he unbuttoned her pants and yanked them to her ankles. In two more moves, he had them flung across the room.

He gazed up at her, the stark, male need in his expression making her glad for the wall behind her. It had been so long since anyone had looked at her like this.

No, not like this. Dailon had viewed her with lust, but it had seemed...tamer somehow. Maybe because her virginity had sat between them like a chaperone. He'd been willing to fool around, but he was less willing to "foul an angel."

The memory of Dailon pricked her heart. Maybe now wasn't the time to do this. "Cipher—"

His warm mouth covered her mound through the silk of her panties, and she had to bite her tongue to keep from shouting. Okay, she was wrong. This *was* the time to do it, and she moaned as his tongue probed her valley, the dampness from his licks blending with her wet arousal. He stroked her with his tongue, and at the rasp of sensation across her clit she rocked her hips and let out a strangled sound as the first tremors of bliss snuck up on her.

But he denied her, the bastard, his impish gaze catching hers as he sliced a fang through the elastic leg of her panties. An erotic growl rolled in his throat as he spread her legs roughly, splitting the fabric with a delicate rip. Now she was open to him, her hot flesh exposed to the cool air and his gaze. Her face went hot and her instinct was to close her legs, but he held her prisoner, and she didn't have the willpower to fight it. Especially when he glanced up at her, his blue eyes ablaze.

"You're so beautiful," he said, so reverently she nearly broke down in tears. Holding her with his gaze, he captured her sex in his open mouth and kissed her deep.

"Cipher," she whispered as she threw her head back against the wall and allowed herself to simply feel something other than the cold misery of life in Sheoul. "This is...so...good."

He made a humming sound that vibrated through her flesh, taking her breath and her thoughts. Gripping his hair, she arched into him, riding his lips as they nibbled at her swollen bud. He brushed them from side to side and suckled gently before licking at her with the flat of his tongue as his thumb dipped inside her. Waves of ecstasy pummeled her as he rimmed her opening, spreading her juices and teasing her out.

"Yes," she moaned. "Oh, *yes.*"

She cried out as his tongue carried her over the line, hurling her into orgasmic bliss. Sharp bursts of pleasure spread from her pelvis to her breasts, taking her breath and, nearly, her consciousness.

Her legs went jelly as the climax ebbed, but he caught her, lifting her as he spun her toward the bed. The backs of her legs hit the mattress, and they both tumbled onto it in a messy tangle of limbs. His masculine weight pinned her deliciously, and she wrapped her arms around him as she spread her thighs to accommodate his big body.

Smiling up at him, her gaze locked with his, she wedged her hand between their bodies to tear open his jeans. He shifted, bracing himself on one elbow to allow her access. Her fingers found the outline of his hard length under the fabric, and he gasped as she squeezed him, toying with him before she flicked open the top button.

The click of the button popping accompanied the soft whisper of a cool breeze.

Oh, shit.

She froze, sensing a presence. Cipher's head cranked toward the entrance and he snarled, a bloodcurdling rumble that echoed off her walls.

Son of a bitch.

Lyre didn't need to look to know that Flail was standing in the doorway.

* * * *

Cipher leaped to his feet and put himself between Lyre and Flail, his wings sprouting before he could stop them. But fuck it, they were shielding Lyre from Flail's view as she dressed, and they made a pointed display of *neener-neener, my wings are bigger than yours*. And if he accidentally zapped Flail with one of his uncontrollable weapons, even better.

Petty? Yes. Did he care? No. Because once he had his powers under control, he was going to zap her intentionally and fatally.

"Did I interrupt something?" Flail asked, all fake innocence and wide eyes as Lyre scrambled to throw on her pants. She gestured at the entrance to the apartment. "Lyre, you know you can set wards to protect your place from prying eyes and unwanted visitors, right?" Fake innocence turned into mocking pity. "Oh, I forgot. You can't."

Cipher had no idea what she meant by that, but Lyre's red-faced fury made clear that she knew.

"What do you want, Flail?" He moved toward her, preparing to toss her off the balcony. He wasn't confined in a cell anymore, his wings weren't bound, and he held a hell of a grudge.

An aura of energy bloomed around her. She was prepared for him to attack, which proved she wasn't stupid. "I come bearing good news."

"Let me guess." Cipher stopped, curious enough to hold off tossing her into the abyss below. It would be pointless anyway, given that she could fly. But it would be fun, and like he'd told Lyre, he was operating with a pleasure deficit. Especially since the bitch had interrupted what would have been a *lot* of pleasure. "You're suffering from an incurable disease that will slowly and painfully kill you. Is that it? Because that would be *great* news."

She didn't look amused. She'd always been lacking in the humor department. "Sorry to disappoint you, but this might be even better. You've earned Bael's trust. To some degree," she amended. "He has an assignment for you."

"Okay, I'll bite," he said, his voice laced with skepticism. "Why the sudden change of heart?"

"Your list panned out." Cipher's gut hit the floor as Flail plopped down on the leather sofa and kicked her feet up on the makeshift coffee table made from an old crate. "We took out one of Azagoth's children. Nearly got a second, but the damned Memitim arrived and ruined everything."

Oh...damn. Oh, fuck. Oh...*fuck!*

Cipher's knees went liquid, and he had to force himself to stay upright. To pretend he wasn't affected by the news. But in reality, he wanted to puke.

He was responsible for an innocent child's death. And not just any child. Azagoth's child. An angel.

"Anyway, congratulations. You've proven your worth." She tossed him the flash drive he'd downloaded the damned list onto. He wanted to step on it. Break it. Smash it to bits. "That contains the names of a few of Bael's enemies. He wants you to devise a computer virus that will kill them. He also wants a virus that will spread through the human population. Something gruesome. Can you make zombies?"

Still sick to his stomach, he stared blindly at the drive. "That's not how computer viruses work." His voice was flat, numb, and he hoped Flail didn't notice.

"You'll make them work. We have confidence in your abilities. And your wings will help you."

His wings? "What will help me is my laptop and access to the internet and demonweb."

"That," Flail said with a knowing smile, "is not an option. You can use your laptop, but it stays where it is. If you need access to the webs, Bael's is available to you."

Screw Bael's devices. No doubt the fallen angel was watching every keystroke on every computer in the region. But Cipher made sure his computer was unhackable and essentially invisible on a network.

"Now," she said as she came to her feet. "I have Memitim to hunt. Azagoth *will* join our cause, or he'll lose everything he loves."

"You *bitch.*"

Uncontrollable rage slammed into him. He knew he should control it. Knew he couldn't let these evil fucks know that he still gave a shit about his old life. His old friends. But knowing they'd killed an innocent child and were still planning to kill Azagoth's offspring boiled off all his logic and laid-back nature.

Opening himself up to the evil surrounding him, he roared in ecstasy and fury as the oily burn of malevolence seeped into his cells. Then he struck out at Flail with whatever fallen angel ability surfaced first.

A stream of fire shot from his palm, but Flail blocked it with an invisible shield. He changed tacks, pummeling her defense with a series of ice shards. She fell back under the intense assault, but suddenly his powers went crazy, and the shards turned into fucking snowballs that burst into acid powder on contact. Powder that burned holes in Lyre's floor, walls, and ceiling, but didn't do a damned thing to Flail or her shield.

"Is that all you can do, Cipher?"

"You'd better hope so," he ground out.

Grinning victoriously, Flail raised her hand to deliver what would probably have been a devastating strike, but Lyre charged, throwing herself into the other female. Flail, caught off guard by the attack, stumbled, and a heartbeat later, she disappeared over the balcony with a scream.

"Ward the opening," he shouted, remembering too late that apparently Lyre couldn't do that. He cursed, unsure how to do it himself.

Turned out that there was no need. Flail rose up in flight, gave them a jaunty wave, and disappeared into the dark sky.

Trembling with rage, adrenaline, and frustration, he shot her the finger. She was going to kill Memitim, and he was helpless to so much as warn Azagoth.

"Damn, I hate her," Lyre snapped, her gaze locked in the direction Flail had gone.

"She needs to die."

Lyre turned to him, her fangs bared. "Then maybe you should get to work on those viruses," she suggested, the silver in her eyes darkening into gunmetal death. It was sexy as hell, and his evil side, growing larger every time he opened himself up to it, stirred.

Simmer down, buddy. We have fallen angels to kill.

That seemed to satisfy his inner sex fiend, and he reached for his uneaten sandwich. A guy had to keep up his energy, after all.

"I'm ready when you are," he said. "Let's go make a plague."

Chapter Thirteen

"Please, my lord, I've told you everything!"

The demon screamed, blood bubbling from his parched, swollen lips, as Azagoth wrenched the horn out of his skull with a wet crack of bone and flesh.

"That was the last one." Azagoth tossed the bloody length of ivory to the floor, where it clattered to rest against another horn. "The next protruding body part I rip off will be located a little farther south. So tell me what I want to know."

The demon moaned, slumping from exhaustion and the strain of hanging by his bony wrists from Azagoth's favorite torture rack. A gift from Malachi, a powerful demon from the Islith region of Sheoul, the mahogany rack was a thing of beauty, perfectly sized to grace the far wall in his office, and conveniently located next to the soul tunnel. This Croucher demon had not, however, come through the tunnel, his soul escorted by a *griminion*.

Nope, his sons Journey and Maddox had dragged the bastard in themselves.

Azagoth's cell phone beeped from his desk. Inconvenient timing, but he swore to Lilliana that he would always get back to her immediately, especially now that she was close to giving birth.

"Hey, Hawk," he called over his shoulder. "Is that a text from Lilli?"

Hawkyn had arrived a few minutes ago with news about Cipher. Somehow, he and Journey had been able to crack into Bael's demonweb, and they'd left a message for the fallen angel. So far, there'd been no response.

Azagoth wasn't sure what to think about Cipher's situation. Bael had taken Cipher for a reason, and Azagoth suspected the kidnapping had something to do with him. Lilliana had pointed out that Unfallen angels everywhere were, in general, being hunted and forced into Sheoul, and that was true. Demons and fallen angels everywhere were preparing for the End of Days now that there was a time table.

But Cipher's abduction had felt personal, because no one in their right mind would abduct anyone under Azagoth's protection.

Which meant that whoever had done it wanted Azagoth's attention.

Azagoth was going to show them why drawing his attention was a very bad thing.

Hawkyn flipped Azagoth's phone over and glanced at the screen. "Yup, it's Lilliana. She wants to know what time to plan for dinner. She's got a recipe of Suzanne's she wants to try on you. Says it's...oh, I see. She wants to try it *on* you." Hawk's face went crimson as he put the phone down and backed away as if it were a poisonous Croix viper. "She's very graphic about it."

Azagoth laughed. Damn, it felt right to do that again. At least, it felt right to be laughing at anything good and pure and pleasant. The only thing that had been funny while Lilliana was gone was the suffering of people who deserved it.

"Suzanne recently did an episode about aphrodisiacs and food," Azagoth said. "Lilliana thought it was interesting."

Hawk cringed the way he always did when his sister and sex came up in the same conversation. Azagoth got that. Suzanne was his daughter, so he didn't like to go there either.

"I don't want to know." Hawkyn gestured to the demon. "Shouldn't you be torturing that guy anyway?"

"I didn't think this was your kind of thing." Not all of Azagoth's offspring had inherited his special interests. Maddox and Emerico showed promise, though.

Hawkyn's expression turned dark. "The bastard tried to kill one of my sisters. The sooner we know who he works for, the sooner we can destroy them."

Azagoth nodded in approval. Maddox had said something similar when he'd asked to stay for the Croucher's interrogation. He'd been disappointed when Mad was called away to watch over one of his

Primori.

He turned back to the demon. "So," he said, as he watched his hands form the claws that were going to do the ripping he'd promised, "are you still insisting that you and your demon buddies just happened to stumble upon my daughter while you were innocently roaming the streets after a night of terrorizing humans? That you didn't know I was Gretchen's father?"

Azagoth had never met Gretchen, one of his young children who had been raised in the human realm, but she was safe in Sheoul-gra now, and once she was settled in and had gotten over the shock she'd been through, he'd introduce himself.

Fear flickered in the demon's eyes as Azagoth dragged one sharp claw down his skeletal chest.

Lower, and the demon began to tremble. Lower, and he swallowed hard, the veins in his scrawny throat bulging.

Lower.

"Okay, okay," the demon blurted, his eyes wild now.

Azagoth dug his claw into the soft abdominal skin. "Okay...what?"

"W-we were sent to kill her," he said in a rush, and now they were finally getting somewhere. "But we didn't know she was your daughter! I swear!"

That was most likely true. It would be stupid to tell underlings too much, especially if the information might make them balk at following an order.

"I believe you," Azagoth said in a pleasant, calm voice. He even paused his finger, letting the demon relax for a moment. Letting him feel hope.

Hope was for fucking morons. This creature was going to die a terrible, painful death, no matter what.

Obviously.

"How unlucky for you that Memitim are rounding up all of my children in the human realm, and Gretchen was next in line." They'd gotten to her just in time. Five minutes later, and her body would probably have been found partially eaten and dumped in a German forest or field. "But you can change your luck." He leaned in, baring his fangs as he lowered his voice to a husky whisper. "Tell me who sent you to kill my daughter."

Silence hung in the air, and for a long moment, Azagoth thought the demon would refuse. But just as he began to drop his hand to start squeezing things until they popped, the Croucher let out a resigned groan.

"Bael," he rasped. "The fallen angels Bael and his brother, Moloc."

Azagoth went taut. The names weren't surprising; Moloc and Bael had been testing Azagoth's patience for centuries in their quest to find ways to keep souls that rightfully belonged to him. But that wasn't what made anger singe the edges of Azagoth's patience as he turned to Hawkyn.

"Bael," he snarled. "The bastard who took Cipher."

"Then this is all connected," Hawkyn said, but he was missing the real link.

Azagoth laid it out, crystal fucking clear. "Cipher has access to the locations of all my human-realm children."

Hawkyn's emerald eyes—Azagoth's eyes—shot wide as the implication sank in. "No way." He shook his head. "*No* damned way. Cipher wouldn't have given Bael anything."

"Are you certain?"

"Yes. I know it," Hawk insisted. "He would never betray us. He'd never betray *you*."

Hawkyn was so convinced of his friend's innocence. Azagoth wished he could be as sure. Or even a little sure. Cipher had been an asset, and he'd been loyal. But in Azagoth's thousands of years of life, he'd seen loyal people turn. Everyone had a price...or a breaking point.

Someone banged on the door. "Hawkyn! Father!"

The urgency in Journey's voice raised the hair on the back of Azagoth's neck. With a mental flick of his mind, the heavy office door swung open.

"What is it?" he asked as Journey rushed inside.

"It's Amelia," Journey breathed.

"Who?"

"Amelia," Hawkyn repeated miserably. "Dammit."

"She is—was—one of your...ah...fuck." Journey dropped his gaze to the floor and Azagoth's gut went with it. He knew where this was going. "She was a sister in the human realm. I was with Jasmine. We went to get her. She...she was the last one on the list. She's dead."

Sudden rage turned Azagoth's blood to acid. Everything inside him burned as he rounded on Hawkyn.

"Still think this is a coincidence?" His voice was warped, spoken through clenched teeth. "Find Cipher. Find him *now*."

"But Father—"

Azagoth's inner demon clawed at his control, and he wasn't in the frame of mind to restrain it. The monster was about to be loosed.

"I offer this one mercy, my son," he growled. "Find Cipher. Find him and kill him. Because if you don't, I will." His sons just stood there. "*Go!*"

They scrambled out of the office, and Azagoth let his beast loose. He was going to break some rules and people were going to pay for killing his children. Eyes for eyes.

He started with the Croucher's.

Chapter Fourteen

In the hour it took for Lyre and Cipher to get from her place to his computer, Cipher's fury had dulled enough that he could temporarily relegate his part in Azagoth's child's death to the background.

Revenge, though, was very much in the foreground.

He fired up his laptop with the single-minded focus of a vampire on the trail of a bleeding human.

"Do you think you can do it?" Lyre asked as she locked the door behind them.

"What, write a virus? Sure."

"The kind of viruses Bael wants?"

Cipher let out a bitter laugh. "No. People have been trying since the internet began."

"But there are stories about people being possessed or cursed after opening emails or files."

He nodded, familiar with those. He'd written code for dozens of types of viruses like that, but as a powerless Unfallen he'd lacked the ability to execute them. Now, maybe he could. They'd be perfect to kill individuals like the enemies Bael wanted dead.

"Those are useful for individuals, but they're limited in scope and expire quickly. Not to mention that the spells can be broken by deleting the emails or closing out the app or whatever. But Bael also wants me to create an enchanted computer virus that can spread from the computer to the human world, and then keep on spreading. It can't be done."

At least, he hoped not.

"Then what are you doing? You said you were going to make a plague."

He'd said that, but really, he was going to *cause* a plague. Because once Azagoth knew Bael was behind his children's deaths, Azagoth was going to become an epidemic. All Cipher needed to do was hide a message inside one of the viruses meant for Bael's enemies. When the virus activated, a subprogram would deliver a warning to Azagoth via the demonweb. Bael would never know.

"Cipher?"

Oh, right. He was supposed to answer her. Probably shouldn't tell her his real plans. He opened his mouth to spew some bullshit he hoped she'd buy. But before he could say anything, his wings sprouted from his back, wrenching and twisting with so much force that he grunted in pain.

"What is it?" Lyre rushed toward him. "What's going on?"

"I don't know," he gritted out. "They popped out on their own and—"

He broke off as an electric tingle sizzled across the surface of his skin and pinprick points of light filled his vision.

"What the hell..?" Transparent cyan glyphs appeared before his eyes. Random numbers, letters, and symbols took shape in the air, some skimming the floor and hugging the ceiling. Holy shit.

"It's code," he whispered.

"Code? Ciph? Are you okay?"

Ciph. She'd called him by his nickname. Felt intimate. Felt...right.

And that was so not what he should be concentrating on right now. No, the programming language floating around was way more significant.

Because weird.

He blinked. Maybe he was hallucinating. What had Lyre said was in the sandwiches? Demon beef and hellrats? Maybe they'd gone bad.

"Hey, Lyre...how old were those sandwiches?"

"I bought them yesterday." She frowned. "Why?"

Closing his eyes, he shook his head. Maybe he could reset his operating system. But nope, when he opened his eyes again, the atmospheric graffiti was still there.

"Can you see this?" he asked.

Lyre glanced around. "See what?"

"The symbols." He pointed at a group of them. "The greenish-blue symbols."

She looked right through them and then turned to him like he'd lost his mind. "I don't see anything. What's going on? You're weirding me out."

"I don't know. It's language of some sort."

"Language? Like a demon language?"

"Like programming language." As he watched, character sets and entities rearranged themselves. A Greek omega symbol spun into a tilde operator squiggly mark and caused a cascade of code into lined formation. "Holy shit," he breathed, as what he was witnessing started to make sense. "It's a spell. Fuck me, I'm *seeing* a spell!"

"How can you see a spell?" She grabbed his arm to get his attention, but he couldn't look away. "What kind of spell?"

"I don't know." It was fascinating how the symbols unique to demonic computer language vibrated while the others were static. "I'm not even sure how I know it's a spell. Or maybe a curse." He remembered a theory he'd hashed out with Hawkyn, and he finally looked down at her. "You know, some people believe that everything in the universe is really made up of mathematical code, and if you could just see and access it, you could control it. Reprogram it. Delete it."

"That's insane." She frowned, appearing to rethink that. "Do you think it's true?"

"I didn't," he admitted. "But I also didn't believe that active spells had source code, either." This was so crazy. Was it his unique fallen angel ability? If so, it was majorly awesome.

"Well, what's the spell you're seeing?" Lyre moved toward a book shelf. "Maybe one of the books is enchanted."

He glanced over at the books, and sure enough, tiny rows of code surrounded a leather-bound tome lying on its side. But that wasn't related to the millions of lines of programming language floating in the room.

"Dammit, I need access to the internet. If I can just plug some of this into the translator I stored in my cloud—" He sucked in a harsh breath, his mind reeling at the sudden clarity. "It's the spell that blocks internet access."

Lyre wheeled around, and he cursed his stupidity at blurting it out. He kept forgetting she was the enemy.

She doesn't feel like the enemy.

No, she didn't. But Flail hadn't felt like an enemy either...until it was too late.

"You're kidding," she said, and just as he was about to say that yes, he was full of shit, she added, "Can you break it?"

Well, that was unexpected. "Are you asking me to?"

"Yes, of course. You can put it back, right? Cipher, this is your gift." Her excitement made him wonder what hers was. "You need to practice with it."

"So Bael can force me to use it? Yeah, great."

She hissed and grabbed his arm. "Bael can never know about this. Never tell anyone about your gifts. Especially not someone like Bael."

"You're not going to tell him?" He looked at her sideways. "I can't believe he didn't tell you to report every one of my abilities to him."

"He did," she admitted. "But what he doesn't know won't hurt him."

Oh, yes it would. Cipher swore it.

"You don't like your boss much, do you?" As he waited for her answer, he concentrated on a few individual characters in the code, using his thoughts in an attempt to rearrange them.

Nothing. Maybe the spell was voice activated.

Lyre plopped down on a fur-lined ice bench. "I hate him."

They could start a club. "Then why are you working for him?" He studied the code and considered another tack. "And what's the Sheoulic word for delete?"

"*Altun.* And I'm working for him because I want revenge on the people who got me expelled from Heaven."

"Yeah, I get that," he said. "But why a deranged lunatic like Bael? Why not a regular lunatic like Revenant?"

"Because the people I want revenge on are in Heaven, and Heaven backs Revenant."

He looked over at her as she kicked her slender legs up on the bench. Legs he'd been between just an hour ago.

Fucking Flail.

"They don't *back* him," he said. "They just prefer him over Satan."

She gave a dismissive snort. "Same thing."

No, it wasn't. Heaven needed allies like Revenant, but from what he'd heard, the Powers That Be didn't interfere with his rule. If Revenant wanted to help someone get revenge on an angel, Heaven might be miffed, but ultimately, they needed him.

Okay, maybe they backed him.

Not wanting to admit she was right, he focused again on the code, choosing a random ampersand as his victim. "*Altun!*"

The code just laughed at him. Well, not literally, but it felt that way.

Sighing, he turned back to Lyre. "So what happens after you get your revenge?"

"What do you mean?"

"I mean, what do you want to do with your life? Spend it helping Bael torment Azagoth? Spend it preparing for Armageddon?"

She drew her knees up to her chest, her expression troubled. "I hadn't really thought that far ahead."

"So you shackled yourself for all eternity to Bael and his empire of evil for the sole purpose of getting revenge and without any thought about what comes after? Seems a little shortsighted."

She glared, the silver in her eyes glinting like daggers. "Well, hello, did you think about the consequences of ruining a Primori before you did it? Or were you bent on your own self-gratification or self-destructiveness?"

"Touché," he muttered. "But in my defense, I never said I wasn't a hypocrite." That coaxed a smile from her, but it was distant. He'd touched a nerve. Maddox insisted that was the best time to keep pressing for information. Cipher had always found the opposite to be true, but hey, he'd give it another shot. "So, this is off topic, but what did Flail mean when she said you couldn't set wards?"

"Nothing," she said with a jerky shrug. "It's just not my skill set."

Seemed odd. Wards were the most basic kind of conjuration there were. Sure, he didn't know how to set one, but that was because he'd only had access to his fallen angel powers for a day. He should have a firm grasp on them within another day or two. Lyre should have obtained the knowledge years ago.

"So how's your progress?" She jumped to her feet. Clearly, she was ready to talk about something else. "Were you able to delete any of the code?" When he shook his head, she cocked hers and asked, "Can you touch it?"

"I tried earlier. My hand passed through it." He suddenly remembered how he used to manipulate 3-D programs in Heaven, and an idea came to him. "But maybe I don't need to *touch* them."

His wings quivered as he summoned energy to his fingertips and reached out as if trying to swat at a group of characters. They vibrated, and he held his breath as he tried again, harder this time.

Yes!

Three numbers and a demonic glyph spun away from the main group and hung in the air. Refocusing his objective from manipulating symbols to obliterating them, he pointed at each line of code and watched as they broke apart and dissolved into sparkly glitter.

"I did it!"

Lyre sat up straight. "We have the internet in here now?"

He blasted the last remaining lines of code. "We should." He turned to his computer and searched for a connection. When the signal lit up, he let out a whoop. "We have active demonweb, baby."

Excited, hopeful for the first time in months, he went straight for his private inbox. Junk. Junk. More junk.

And an email from Hawk, dated seven months ago.

We're looking for you.

That was all. Four words. But those four words meant everything.

Another one from Hawk, dated six months ago.

We're looking for you.

There were more, one each month, ensuring he'd know they hadn't given up. But it was the most recent one that had his heart pumping a mile a minute.

We found you. Flip the bedora gateway switch.

He grinned like a lunatic. Hawkyn and Journey had hacked into Bael's private network and given Cipher a way to shut down his security system. Cipher just had to access it.

"Um...Cipher? What's going on?"

He looked up, alarmed by the urgency in Lyre's voice. The walls, once opaque, were growing transparent, and suddenly a klaxon rang out.

The code...oh, damn, oh, *shit!*

"I missed the failsafe." How could he have been so stupid?

"What?"

His fingers flew over the keyboard. He had to get a message out. Fast. "There was code in the spell that triggers an alarm if the spell is broken."

The door burst open, and armored guards, their weapons drawn, spilled inside.

He. Was. Fucked.

Chapter Fifteen

Lilliana smiled into her laptop's camera as her friend Cara held up baby Aleka. "I know I've only been back in Sheoul-gra for a couple of days, but I swear she's grown."

Cara cradled the infant, swaddled in a blanket made from the golden wool of Heavenly sheep, in the crook of her arm as she tenderly stroked her rosy cheek. "I think so too."

Longing stirred in Lilliana's chest as she smoothed her palm over her belly. She couldn't wait to hold her own child in her arms. Only a month to go. She and Cara had conceived within days of each other, but as an angel Lilliana had an extra four to five weeks of gestation.

"Well, you both look amazing," she said. "I'm so glad you got a chance to call."

"I just wish you were here." Cara sighed. "I miss having you around. Maleficent misses you too. She's been searching the island for you, and she won't stop whining."

Guilt and sorrow made Lilliana's heart clench. Poor Mal must feel so abandoned. "Maybe you should send her here. I'm sure Azagoth will be okay with it. It's not like hellhounds don't haunt the Inner Sanctum anyway."

"You sure?" At Lilliana's nod, Cara continued. "How *are* things going with Azagoth? I've been dying to know what he did when he saw you."

"I thought he'd be angry," Lilliana said. "But he understood why I left and why I didn't tell him I was pregnant."

That wasn't entirely the truth, since they hadn't talked about it yet. Azagoth hadn't brought it up, but he'd also been really busy. *The talk* was coming, and she knew it.

"So what was his reaction when he first saw you?"

Lilliana's cheeks burned. "He was, um, shocked..."

"And then..?"

"And then he flew me up to the balcony and tore my clothes off."

"He did not!" Cara laughed. "Wow. That sounds deliciously scandalous and totally like something Ares would do after not seeing me for nine months. How does he feel about the baby?"

Lilliana heard the thud of footsteps behind her and knew it was Azagoth. Her bodyguard stationed outside the door would never have allowed anyone else inside. A heartbeat later, Azagoth's deep voice echoed through the room.

"I can't wait for our son or daughter to arrive," he said, as his hands came down on Lilliana's shoulders.

She reached up and laid her hand over his. He'd been so affectionate and attentive since she'd been back. Even better, he'd been open in a way he hadn't been even before his emotions had gone out of control.

"Well," Cara said, "I'll let you two spend some time together." She wrinkled her nose. "I think someone needs a diaper change anyway." She glanced at Azagoth and laughed. "I just pictured the big bad Grim Reaper changing a nappy. That'll keep me in a good mood for the rest of the week." She waved. "Talk to you later!"

After the screen went dark, Lilliana spun in her chair to face Azagoth. He looked so handsome in casual clothes, his black jeans, charcoal Henley, and combat boots giving him a relaxed air that no one would mistake for anything less than lethal danger.

"This was a nice surprise," she said. "To what do I owe this visit?"

"It was time for a break and I wanted to see you." His deep emerald eyes grew serious. "I think it's time to talk."

Oh. She hadn't been looking forward to this. At all. "You want to know why I didn't tell you I was pregnant."

He sank down on the chaise lounge she used for reading, his legs spread, his forearms resting on his knees. "I know why you left, but I don't know why you kept this from me."

She fidgeted in her seat as she thought about what to say. It was weird; every day while she was in Greece she'd prepared for what she'd say to him. Went over and over it in her head. And now she was drawing a blank.

"I guess..." She inhaled, bracing herself. "I guess at first it was just too soon. I wanted you to sort out your issues without having anything else to think about. So I decided to tell you when I started showing, but every time I talked to you, I just...couldn't. You were so worried about all your children. So many were in danger, and then you said we were never going to have one together...I got nervous."

He sat in silence for a long moment. "I remember that," he said quietly. "Maddox and Emerico were being assholes, and then Meera was killed." His voice went low, taking on a smoky tone. "It was a bad day." He reached over and took her hand. "But I was wrong. There is nothing I want more than you and our child in my life, and I swear to you, I will do everything within my power to make sure you're both safe."

"I know," she said. "And I know someone murdered one of your young sons inside Sheoul-gra, and you're freaked out. But is the bodyguard really necessary? You said yourself that the murderer had to be a fallen angel, and you kicked all of them out."

The only fallen angels who remained were his trusted assistants and their mates. A handful of Unfallen remained as well, but again, they were the ones who had been with him for years as they tried to work their way back into Heaven, and that wouldn't happen if they were killing his children.

"I won't take any chances with you." His words were clipped, forceful, and she knew arguing was pointless. She wasn't going to win this battle, and ultimately, having a shadow wasn't *too* annoying.

"Okay." Resolved to her fate, she squeezed his hand. "For what it's worth, I'm sorry I didn't tell you about the baby. But," she added, "I don't regret leaving. I needed to go. And you needed it too."

A low growl rattled his chest. "I fucking hate that you're right."

She laughed as she brought his hand to her lips. This had gone better than she could have even hoped for. "Why don't you take the rest of the day off? I can fire up the *chronoglass* and take us someplace warm and sunny and private."

"Maybe later," he said, shooting her a playful wink that spoke volumes about his mood. Usually his brand of playful was the cat-toying-with-a-mouse variety. "I have some VIP souls coming in."

"VIP souls?"

A shadow flickered in his eyes and he smiled, a morbid, malicious smile that sent a chill down her spine. "Sons of Moloc and Bael. Princes of their territories."

She gasped in disbelief. "What? How? Did you send *griminions* for them?"

"*Griminions* only reap souls. They don't kill." His smile grew even darker. "I sent souls from the Inner Sanctum."

This time her breath clogged in her throat, trapped there momentarily by the intensity of her shock. "Isn't it forbidden to release souls if they aren't reincarnated?"

"It's not forbidden if Heaven doesn't find out." She could argue that it was still forbidden, but his phone beeped, and he dug it from his pocket. "You disapprove?"

"No, of course not," she said fiercely. "Moloc and Bael are monsters who had your children murdered. Their sons are fair game." She paused. "They *are* evil, right?"

"What is it Journey says? Mucho evil? They're that." He grinned at the phone. "They're here."

"What are you going to do with them?" As if she couldn't guess. He was going to play cat and mouse.

"Do you really want to know?"

Not really, but Azagoth's secretive nature was one of the reasons she'd left, and during the months when they'd spoken via Skype, she'd made clear that while she didn't need to know gory details, she didn't want to be "protected" from what he truly was.

"I assume you're going to torture them into telling you why their fathers are killing your children." At his nod, she asked, "Do you have any theories?"

"I suspect they're plotting a coup and want me to play a role in freeing Satan and destroying Revenant."

Well, that wasn't cool. "What are you going to do if you're right?"

"The same thing I'll do if I'm wrong." He shoved to his feet and pulled her with him. "No matter what, Bael and Moloc are going to die."

* * * *

It sucked that destroying souls came with a cost, but fortifying Satan with a drop of strength was a price Azagoth was more than willing to pay today. Bael and Moloc's sons had been monsters, but more than that, their darkness would return to Satan, and that bastard would know

Azagoth was responsible. It was a message of sorts, a *fuck you* that could only be better if Azagoth had destroyed Satan's offspring instead.

An hour later, Azagoth was still burning a serious soul-destroyer high as he entered his library, where Hawkyn was pacing a hole in the floor while waiting for him.

"I heard from Cipher," Hawk said before Azagoth had even shut the door.

"Heard from him? You were supposed to kill him." Hawkyn was lucky Azagoth was in a good mood, because he really, really wanted Cipher dead.

Hawkyn held out his phone. "He sent this. I think he was in a hurry, but I got the gist."

The list is out. Save the kids. Bael is after Memitim.

Azagoth rolled his eyes. "He's evil, son. You can't trust him."

"You're evil too," Hawkyn pointed out.

"Exactly. I will fuck over anyone who gets in my way or who tries to harm what's mine. I will lie, cheat, and kill. There is no line I will not cross. Do you not think Cipher would do the same?"

"He hasn't been a True Fallen for long. He's not lost to us." He took his phone back and scrolled. "He also says he thinks he can bring down the wards that prevent *griminions* from entering when he takes out the security system with the bug Journey planted."

He hadn't known about a security system bug, but it didn't really matter. The wards thing was curious, though. Bael and Moloc's ability to keep the *griminions* at bay had meant that no souls had been reaped from their territories in decades. Not even the souls Azagoth had released from Sheoul-gra to grab the fallen angels' sons had been able to enter. They'd had to take the males while they were fucking around in other regions of Sheoul.

"When can Cipher do this?" Azagoth asked.

"I don't know. I've tried contacting him, but he's not replying."

There was a tap at the door, and Z's voice boomed from behind the thick wood. "I just got word that Reaver and Revenant are on their way."

Before Z even stopped talking, Azagoth's bones vibrated like a tuning fork, and a blast of nuclear energy slammed into him. They were here. Fuck. He wasn't in the mood. He was never in the mood when it came to dealing with those douchebags.

"I'll go." Hawkyn beelined for the door, anxious to either miss

Reaver and Revenant, or to get away from Azagoth before he told him to kill Cipher again. Maybe both. "I'll let you know if I hear from Ciph."

He whipped open the door, and lo and behold, the Prince of Heaven and the King of Hell were standing right there in the doorway.

They exchanged brief nods, and then Reaver and Revenant strode inside.

"Well, well," Azagoth said. "If it isn't the Wonder Twins."

"The what?" Revenant asked.

"A brother sister superhero team from Saturday morning cartoons," Reaver explained. "Back when I was Unfallen, Wraith made me watch a lot of those things."

"That's cool," Revenant said. "We didn't have fun shit like cartoons in the part of Hell where I grew up."

Reaver shot his brother a look of exasperation. "You just can't let that go, can you?"

Revenant shrugged in his black leather duster. "It's still a sore spot." He plopped down in the overstuffed chair by the fire.

"That's my seat," Azagoth said. "Move."

"Whatever, Sheldon." Holding up his hands, Revenant scooted to the couch. At Reaver's quizzical expression, Rev shrugged again. "I like sitcoms. Sue me."

"Are you two done?" Azagoth asked. Talk about exasperation. "Maybe you could tell me why you're here?"

Reaver turned to him, his body taut, his expression serious. "I'm here to warn you not to push the boundaries of your limits, which were agreed upon in the Sheoul-gra Accord."

"What he said." Revenant kicked his booted feet up on the coffee table, as relaxed as Reaver was strung tight.

"This must be serious if Heaven is sending its most powerful angel and Sheoul's overlord."

Revenant barked out a laugh. "Heaven doesn't *send* me anywhere, Soul Man. I'm here because this concerns my realm too."

The fire in the hearth snapped and hissed as Reaver waved his palm over the flames. Did he notice that the fire burned hot? It had been cold for months, its flames pale blue, reflecting Azagoth's heart while Lilliana had been gone.

He hated that his environment was so connected to his moods, that he could be so easily read by those with an observant eye or half a brain.

Reaver turned away from the fire. "You released souls into Sheoul," he said, getting right to it. "The Angelic Council is apoplectic. So we're here to tell you to knock it the hell off."

"Fuck the council," Azagoth growled. "Bael has been killing my children. I have the right to defend my family."

"Only within the confines of Sheoul-gra."

Azagoth gave a bitter laugh. He'd been stupid to agree to such restrictive rules. "What would you do, Reaver? What would you do if Bael killed Limos? Or Logan? Or any of your children or grandchildren? Would you sit around in Heaven and do nothing, simply because you signed a piece of parchment? You, who haven't followed a rule...ever?"

"There's not a rule I wouldn't break for my family," Reaver said.

"But you can't be all blatant about it," Revenant broke in. "If you're going to do the revenge thing, use your *griminions*. No one would know. But man, you release souls, and it sets off seismic alarms."

"I don't really give a shit about the souls." Reaver shoved Revenant's feet aside and sat on the opposite end of the couch. "The Angelic Council needs to chill out. But Bael...he can't die."

"Oh, he can die," Azagoth promised. He *would* die. Soon.

"I mean that he needs to *stay* alive."

As if that was going to happen. Still, he should probably know the reasoning behind Reaver's ridiculous announcement. "I give. Why should Bael keep breathing?"

Reaver looked troubled. "I don't know."

"You don't know?" Azagoth stared at the angel. "Then why the fuck—"

"The Moirai summoned him," Revenant announced in a bored tone, as if the Moirai, legendary angelic seers who weren't allowed to speak to anyone except in the most dire of circumstances, had casually asked Reaver to tea.

Hell, until now, Azagoth had actually suspected they were a myth. Sequestered angels who lived on another plane and in all timelines at the same time? Yeah, bullshit.

Except, apparently, it wasn't.

"They see instability in the current timeline," Reaver said. "They stressed that Bael's demise would cause even more destabilization."

"And why do I give a shit about the destabilization of a timeline I know nothing about and that clearly favors Heaven in the Final Battle and beyond?"

"I'm wondering the same thing, bro," Rev said. "If something's good for Heaven, that means it's bad for me."

"Not when we have a common goal, and that's to keep Satan from winning the Final Battle."

"Yeah, well, I don't give a fuck what your Fates have to say." When Reaver cursed, Azagoth held up his hand to stay the lecture. "Take it easy, Halo. Bael doesn't have to die for me to get my revenge. I can keep him alive and in agony for all eternity."

Revenant stood, a big grin on his face. "I knew I liked you."

Azagoth looked between the two. "So are we cool?"

"Yeah," Reaver said. "But watch it. I don't give a shit what you do, but I have to be the bad guy when the Angelic Council gets a bug up their collective asses."

"Come on, bro." Revenant opened the door. "I'm jonesing for a burger."

Reaver was all about a fast food lunch, and they got out of there without so much as a goodbye.

The moment they were gone, he called out, "Lilli? I know you're there."

The hidden panel at the back of the library slid open, and a sheepish, gorgeous, pregnant angel stepped out. "I'm sorry. I didn't mean to eavesdrop. I slipped away to see you and heard you guys talking."

"You just felt the sudden need to use the secret passage to come to the library?" He gave her a *don't bullshit me* look. "You were ditching your bodyguard, weren't you?"

She had the good grace to blush. "Maybe."

She walked over to him, her hands on her belly. Beneath her palm, the baby moved, and when he reached out to feel the movement, his heart stuttered at the instant connection that formed between him and the child.

"Is Grim Junior talking to you again?"

He cocked an eyebrow. "Grim Junior?"

"Do you hate it?"

"Yes."

Her laugh filled his office and his heart. It was so good to have her back. "Guess we should talk about names then, no?"

"Soon," he promised. "I've got a lot to do right now."

"Revenge does take up a lot of time, I suppose." She glanced at the door Reaver and Revenant had just gone through. "They seemed to want to put a damper on your plans to get it. What are you going to do?"

"What do you think, my darling?" He palmed her cheek and stroked her smooth skin with his thumb. He'd never take touching her for granted again. "I'm going to ignore everything they said and kill Bael, of course."

And he dared Heaven to try to stop him.

Chapter Sixteen

The antechamber outside Bael's great hall was freezing. Not that Lyre experienced cold the way humans did, what with all the teeth-chattering, hypothermia, and death. But it was still pretty uncomfortable, and when combined with the terror of what might lie ahead, she couldn't help but shiver.

Bael had made her wait out here for almost twelve hours. Cipher's fate was still unknown. The one bright spot in the day had come when one of his minions had brought news of his son's death at Azagoth's hands. Bael's roars of fury and his murder of the messenger had given her the most pleasure she'd experienced in a long time.

Finally, the great hall's massive doors opened, and Bael's Ramreel guard gestured for her to enter.

She did her best to control her breathing, her pulse, and her sweat glands as she walked across the floor, her boots cracking down on the bones and teeth set into the umber tiles.

"My lord," she said, bowing deeply when she reached the dais where the fallen angel sat on a throne made of more bones and teeth. A set of desiccated angel wings formed the back of the throne, the yellowed feathers dotted with ancient dried blood.

He didn't waste any time. "I just found out that Azagoth murdered my son and my nephew, so I'm in a bad fucking mood. Don't piss me off, Lyre," he warned. "Tell me how Cipher disabled the demonweb block."

"I don't know," she lied calmly, relying on one of the few skills she had that was worth anything down here. "He was using his laptop to work on the viruses you requested, and the next thing I knew, your goons were storming into the room."

"You weren't watching him?"

"Of course I was watching him," she snapped. "But I don't know how all that tech stuff works."

Her answer seemed to mollify him, maybe because it was true. She could operate email and search engines, but everything else was as much of a mystery to her as Stonehenge's purpose was to humans.

Bael sat back in the chair, his narrowed gaze locked on her like a weapon. "Did he create any viruses?"

She shook her head. "He says they're complicated and that it'll take time."

"Time?" He made a sound of derision. "With his computer skills and the plague talent that came with his wings, he should be able to snap his fingers and come up with what I want. He's stalling. He's stalling and I'll kill him! I'll slice him and skin him and..."

He went off on an insane, chaotic tangent, and she knew him well enough to stay silent while he let off some crazy steam.

When he was finally done, having promised to maim and/or kill Cipher in a few dozen ways, she asked tentatively, "How do you know what talents came with his wings? Cipher isn't even aware of all of his abilities yet."

Bael reached into a bowl sitting on the arm of his throne and plucked out something oblong and dripping with clotted blood. Repulsed, she swallowed sickly and hoped to hell that when evil began to flourish inside her she wouldn't develop a taste for disgusting things.

"I know what those wings can do because they aren't Cipher's." He spoke calmly, as if he hadn't just screamed about boiling Cipher until his eyeballs burst. "They belonged to Asher."

"Asher? He was killed last year—" She sucked in a shocked breath, remembering the scars at the base of Cipher's wings. "You cut off his wings, didn't you? You cut them off and transplanted them onto Cipher." So bizarre. "But why?"

Bael popped the bloody bit into his mouth and chewed. "We needed Asher's specific skill set, and Cipher was the perfect recipient."

She shouldn't be surprised, but damn, this was some devious shit. She'd never heard of a wing transplant before. But it explained why Cipher's powers and flying ability were so out of control.

"So how, exactly, will you be using your computer virus?"

Bael crunched on something and swallowed. "Depends on what his viruses do."

"Well, maybe you could write up a wish list," she said sarcastically.

"That's a good idea, my love!" He leaped to his feet, startling her into taking a step back. "Imagine if he could make a virus that would be executable in Heaven." He threw his arms above his head in a show of maniacal exuberance. "Wonderful!" He grinned at her. "That's how you could get your revenge."

Yikes. That would be one hell of a revenge. She wanted her sister and the bastards who condemned her to pay, but setting loose a plague in Heaven could invite destruction on a...well, a biblical scale. For the first time, she wished Moloc was here to temper his brother's insanity.

"Yes," he purred as he took his seat again. "Tell Cipher I want a virus that will affect angels. And another that will affect millions of humans. And yet another that can be sent to individual demons and fallen angels." He closed his eyes as if picturing the mass destruction he was talking about. "I will be the most powerful fallen angel in history."

Aside from Satan, of course. And actually, if Cipher could do all of that, *he* would be the most powerful fallen angel— second to Satan—in history. He could rule the world with that kind of power.

"My lord...if I may." She cleared her throat. "Where is Cipher?"

He blinked as if he'd forgotten the lynchpin in his plan for universal domination. "Ah. Cipher. The Isle of Torture, maybe?" He used one long fingernail to stir the contents of the bowl. "Flail wanted to play with him. If you hurry, you can catch her."

Shit!

She started toward the door, but he called her back.

"Cipher can have access to the demonweb, but only on my network," he said. "My people will watch every move."

"Of course." She turned to leave again.

"And Lyre?"

Her insides turned to jelly at his tone. It was his sadistic one. The one that sounded like a dull knife scraping bone. "Yes, my lord," she whispered.

"You know you belong to me."

She swallowed her loathing and the "Fuck you, you piece of shit," that sat on her lips and instead uttered a mandatory, "Yes, my lord."

For the ten millionth time, she regretted agreeing to serve him in any capacity he wished for all eternity if he helped her get the revenge she craved. She'd been out of her mind with anger and grief, and the implications of *any capacity* and *for all eternity* were, for the first time, truly hitting home.

"*Everything* of yours belongs to me," he said, and her mind instantly flashed to Flail, who must have told him about finding them in bed. "Including your virginity."

He knows? Shock stole her breath, and then a blow to her spine sent her sprawling to the floor and gasping for air. His heavy footsteps fell like thunder, coming closer, threatening destruction.

She tried to push to her feet, but something held her frozen to the floor and she could only watch as Bael's gore-crusted boots stopped next to her head. He bent over, his hot, rancid breath blowing in her ear.

"Betray me in any way, and I will take your virginity with a sword. Do you understand?"

"Y-yes," she gasped.

Her skin crawled as he stroked her hair. "But help me use Cipher to free Satan, and you can be our queen as we serve at his side."

Oh, God. She couldn't have heard him right. "*Our* queen?"

"Moloc and I. We are one." He yanked her to her feet with a painful jerk of her hair and tossed her at the door, where she landed in heap. "Go. Make my viruses."

She had her feet under her and was out the door in a heartbeat.

The Ramreel guard watched her with beady eyes until she got around the corner, where she stumbled to a halt, grabbed her knees, and struggled to catch her breath.

What had she gotten herself into?

Her conversation with Cipher earlier came back to her. Haunting her.

You shackled yourself for all eternity to Bael and his empire of evil for the sole purpose of getting revenge and without any thought about what comes after?

At the time, what he'd said hadn't really sunken in. Her daily life since falling had been about one thing: revenge. But what would happen later? Was becoming some sort of brother-wife demon queen truly what she had to look forward to? Why her? Why wouldn't they choose Flail, who seemed to enjoy the brothers' penchant for vile acts?

And was revenge really even all that important anymore? Merely surviving filled most of her life, and helping Bael try to jumpstart Armageddon filled the rest.

The same impulsivity that had gotten her wings sliced off had gotten her an eternity of hell, and her only hope was that evil would take her so completely that she didn't care anymore. Because right now, she did care.

She was a fallen angel. She should be thrilled to hear of Bael's plans for Satan, Heaven, and her enemies. But this was too much.

This was *way* too much.

This was the kind of shit Flail should be excited about, and if she wanted to—

Flail.

Bael said she'd been heading to see Cipher. Screw that. Cipher was *hers.*

Heart thundering in her chest, Lyre sprinted toward the castle's main exit.

Hold on, Cipher. I'm coming.

* * * *

Of all the beatings Cipher had endured during his time in Sheoul, the ones he'd gotten over the last few hours had been the worst.

Oh, he'd dealt with far more painful, off-the-scale torture, but in his mind, that was different than a beating. A beating involved fists and feet, maybe a blunt object, and a whole lot of taunting.

It was fucking annoying. At least when he was in agony, the pain shut down his brain. But today he'd been hung like a punching bag to endure the chatter of demons who'd used him as practice before they were ushered into the arena for their fights to the death. He was the warm-up.

And he wondered if, at some point, he was going to be tossed in the arena too.

Even as the thought filtered through his battered brain, Flail showed up.

No. Fucking. Way.

Today was not his lucky day.

"Looks like you got yourself into hot water," she said, sounding far too happy about it.

"You know me," he drawled. "Always out of the fire and into the pot."

"Mmm." She flicked the door to the training room closed with her mind. "Is that why you got kicked out of Heaven?"

He wasn't going to tell her jack shit about why he lost his wings.

Weird that he'd spilled all to Lyre, though. Just spit it out like it was no big deal. But then, Lyre hadn't betrayed him or tortured him, so there was that. Plus, he couldn't help but like Lyre. Other than the time she'd fed him to demon fish, she'd been pretty cool. They'd spent months talking about mundane things, like the topography of Bael's territory, the locations of the Harrowgates scattered through his realm, and the best flavor of ice cream.

The ice cream talk wouldn't help get him out of here, but the other shit might. Not that Lyre had given him intel when he'd asked, or even all at once. He'd pieced it together over time, keeping mental notes on anything that might prove useful. But in the course of the information-gathering, he'd learned enough about Lyre to not hate her. And now he actually felt something for her. A protective instinct that made him grateful she hadn't been here while the demons had pounded on him. And that she wasn't here now, when Flail was going to do whatever it was she liked to do. Which he guaranteed wouldn't be something *he* liked to do.

He tested the rope binding his hands as he hung from the ceiling by his wrists. Nothing had changed. The rope held, preventing both escape and his ability to use any of his powers. He couldn't even break the damned rope to get to one of the hundreds of weapons locked on racks around the room.

Too bad, too, because he'd love to shove one of those spears right through Flail's evil heart.

"I guess I'm getting the silent treatment," Flail said as she plucked a dagger from a rack. "I wonder if you can scream in silence."

He already knew the answer to that.

It was no.

The door banged open with such force that a piece splintered and lodged in the wall. Then, in a whirlwind of energy, Lyre burst in like he'd summoned her. Forget wanting her to stay away. She was a badass bundle of fury with lasers for eyes, and it was hot. As. Fuck.

"Get away from him, you bitch."

Yes! Bonus badass points for quoting *Aliens*, intentionally or not.

Flail laughed, but Lyre threw a swing and decked the bitch, cutting her off mid-guffaw. The surprisingly powerful blow sent a couple of Flail's teeth clattering to the ground.

Lyre didn't back off or even slow down. Like a battle-seasoned warrior, she pressed her advantage, swiping a sword from a rack and attacking while Flail was off balance. Flail fell back under the assault, and just as she summoned an elemental sword of her own, a massive blade of fire, Lyre disappeared in a puff of vapor.

What the hell?

Then he saw it. The vapor *was* Lyre. Flail shouted in frustration as she whacked uselessly at the wispy rope of smoke that circled her, taunting her, *laughing* at her. He could actually hear soft giggles as Lyre made a joke out of the other female.

Abruptly, Lyre shot upward and dove down, wrapping her misty form around his wrists.

"No!" Flail ran toward him, but the rope broke and he dropped to the ground, his hands free, power singing through his veins.

Now Flail was going to pay for everything she'd done to him.

And then it was Bael's turn.

Chapter Seventeen

Lyre had had enough of that skank.

So she loved it when Cipher hit the ground, popped his wings, and slammed Flail with a summoned wave of scalding water.

That was a new power. And it was all kinds of awesome.

Flail screamed as her skin blistered and peeled, steam rising from her body. Somehow she managed to strike back with her fire sword, catching Cipher in the ribs. The stench of burnt and boiled flesh mingled in the air like a demon chef was preparing some sort of savory fallen angel soup.

Clutching the cauterized wound, Cipher hit the ground and rolled into Flail, bowling her over and knocking the wind from her lungs. As she gasped for air, Lyre, still in her vapor form, had an idea. Like, why the hell not?

Mind set on a course of action, Lyre darted into Flail's open mouth.

Flail tried to scream, but she was choking and gagging, and Lyre wondered what would happen if she slid right into the bitch's lungs.

Blind to whatever was happening outside Flail's mouth, she squirmed around, plugging the other female's windpipe and making her squeal in rage and panic. There were grunts, flailing, and then everything went still and quiet.

"Lyre?"

Lyre slid between Flail's motionless lips and materialized next to her as she lay on the ground.

There was a spear through her chest.

Awesome.

Cupping the back of Lyre's head, Cipher drew her in for a kiss that was as hot as it was quick. "That was one of the coolest things I've ever seen." His fierce, admiring gaze held hers. "Awesome gift."

She shrugged awkwardly, a little dazed and flustered by his unexpected kiss. Not that she was complaining. He could do that anytime he wanted to.

"It's kind of useless. I can't manipulate things very well. But every once in a while it comes in handy." Which was a good thing since it was pretty much her only fallen angel ability. She gestured to Flail. "She's not going to be unconscious for long."

"I know," he said grimly. "We have to finish her off."

As much as she'd love that, killing Flail right now was impossible.

"We can't. Bael will know as soon as her soul goes to him." She glanced around the room, thinking they could tie her up to buy some time, but when she spotted the coffin-like chest in the corner, she got an idea. "Let's shove her inside the torture casket."

His brow knit together in confusion. "What's a torture casket? I thought that chest was for storing weapons."

"Nope." She grabbed Flail's wrists and started dragging her toward the stone box. "Once you put someone in it, it seals for twelve hours. The poor bastard inside gets twelve hours of terror. Nightmares of the things they're most afraid of."

"Huh. Demons are really creative, aren't they?" He gestured for Lyre to stand back, and then he hauled Flail's unconscious body up over his shoulder. "I'd rather kill her, but I'll just make that a future goal."

"Everyone needs aspirations, I guess." Although it had occurred to her that, beyond revenge, she had none. It made her feel...empty.

He dropped her unceremoniously into the box and slammed the lid closed. The gold lock on the front spun and glowed, and a moment later, Flail's muffled screams assured them it was working.

"Come on." She took Cipher's hand. "We need to get out of here." She stopped, an idea sparking in her brain. "Wait. You were able to see the spell that kept you from accessing the internet. Can you see the one on your wings that keeps you from being able to flash inside Bael's territory?"

He frowned. "I don't know."

As if his wings knew they were talking about them, they flapped crazily, nearly knocking him off his feet. She should probably tell him the truth about them, but right now might not be the best time. He cursed as he tried to get the dead fallen angel's wings under control. Finally they remained still, although they quivered with the effort it must have taken him to keep them that way.

"I can see the spell," he said, "but not all of it." With Flail's cries for help as background noise, he concentrated for a little while, and then shook his head. "I think I need to be able to see the entire code in order to alter it. Dammit. And why the fuck won't my wings behave?"

She started to answer, but at the sound of voices outside the door, she thought better of it. "I'll tell you, but not here. Come on."

Quickly and without incident, she led him out of the building Bael had dedicated entirely to imprisoning and torturing his enemies...and anyone else he felt like slaughtering for fun. As soon as they were outside, they took flight, which went about as well as the last time, with Cipher struggling to maintain altitude and course.

He cursed the entire way to the nearby Valley of Asshole Trees, as she called it, a rift between two volcanoes that had developed into an orchard of spiky trees that produced round blackish-purple fruit. She'd discovered the valley about a year ago, one of the few places in Bael's realm that wasn't completely nightmarish. Even the lizard-monkeys that lived in the trees were kind of cute.

Well, they weren't terrifying carnivores, anyway. That had to count for something.

"What is this place?" Cipher turned in a slow circle on the stubby but lush yellow grass, taking it all in. "It's beautiful. In a weird, grotesque way. Those apples probably eat people, don't they?"

If they did, demons would have found a way to weaponize them by now.

"No, but they're gross. They're like raw hamburger inside. Hell stallions and hell mares love them." Sobering, she looked up at the plume of ash that had puffed out of the top of the one of the distant volcanoes. "Do you want out of here? Out of Bael's realm, I mean. Out of Sheoul."

He pivoted around to her. "Is that a trick question?"

It wasn't, but trying to explain herself wasn't going to be easy, and it took her a moment to put the words together. When she finally did, her voice sounded tired, as if she hadn't slept in years. It felt that way, too.

"I fucked up, Cipher," she sighed. "I don't want any part of Bael and Moloc's plans."

"What plans?"

"All of them." Her fists clenched in anger at the memory of what Bael said he wanted to do to the populations of Earth and Heaven. "I was so pissed off, so hateful after I lost my wings that I wasn't thinking straight. I signed on with Bael and Moloc because I wanted revenge, but you made me rethink that." At the skeptical arch of Cipher's brow, she jammed her fists on her hips. "What, you don't believe me?"

"I want to, but this could be a trick."

Given Flail's betrayal almost a year ago, she understood why he'd think that. "You've seen how I live. What life is like here. How Bael treats people. I have no reason to lie."

"Saving your own skin is a reason," he pointed out. "Revenge is a reason."

A hot, stale wind ruffled his hair and made her long ponytail flutter against her neck. She watched as the breeze knocked a fruit to the ground, where a lizard-monkey snatched it before scampering up the tree.

"I chose the wrong team, Cipher. I should have remained an Unfallen."

"I can see the appeal of entering Sheoul," he admitted. He looked up, his expression thoughtful, his strong, masculine profile nothing short of majestic as he took in the sky made orange by volcanic activity. "As an Unfallen, most angels don't have powers, and those who do got them through sorcery."

"I still don't."

He turned his gaze back to her, and she shivered at the intensity of it. Sometimes he was super laid back, and others, like now, he carried an aura of authority that made her feminine side take notice in the most inopportune ways.

"You still don't what?"

"Have powers." She hated admitting this, but it was time to lay it all on the line. If she wanted out of here, he was her best hope, and he wasn't going to help her if he didn't trust her. "I mean, I have a couple, but they're weak."

"I saw your little vapor trick. That didn't strike me as weak."

"Today it came in handy, but it's mostly useless. I can fit through small cracks and keyholes, but any fallen angel can get past locked doors and stuff like that anyway. Remember I told you never to reveal your unique power? Well, that's mine, and everyone here already knows about it."

She'd been so stupid, so happy to have any ability at all that when it manifested as her very first power, she'd shown it off. In her extreme naïveté, she hadn't realized it would be pretty much her only gift, and that other fallen angels delighted in sharing fellow angels' secrets. Acting on her desire for allies after losing her Heavenly friends and family had been so incredibly foolish.

"You've healed me several times," Cipher pointed out. It was nice of him to try to make her feel better, but it didn't do much good.

"The healing power I used on you? It only worked because your healing abilities were already powerful. I can't set wards. I can barely swat a fly with mental strikes. The one unique ability I have is all but useless."

"Must have been awful to go from being a Heavenly angel to a fallen angel with limited powers."

She laughed bitterly. "You'd think. But I was a weak angel, too. It's why I got assigned as a historian and researcher. You don't need angelic powers for that."

He seemed to think on what she'd said. "So you want to escape Bael's clutches, and you want me to help. Is that what you're saying?"

"I don't deserve your help. But I'm asking for it."

"And then what? You'll want help to get your revenge?"

"I'm over that," she said. "I don't care anymore." For some reason, her eyes stung, and tears welled up.

"Your tears say you do," he said, as he caught a drop with his finger, his touch so gentle it didn't even seem real. Not in a place like this. Not in a Hell realm.

"I think...I think I'm...I don't know." Drawing in a ragged breath, she searched her brain for the right words. "I feel...relieved. Like I don't need to hold on to that anger anymore."

"Yeah, well, I'm still pissed." His wings flared and flapped for no apparent reason. "And these stupid things aren't helping. Seriously, what the fuck?"

"Oh, ah, about that..."

He shot her a *what now* look. "Do not tell me that they're cursed or some shit."

How could she put this gently? "Do you know of a fallen angel named Asher?"

"Why would I—" He broke off, and then nodded. "As an angel, he was from the Order of Thrones. He was lead on the Ten Plagues of Egypt debacle."

"That's the one. Terrible mess. Humans got the stories all wrong." She blew out a breath. "Anyway, after he got the boot, he joined up with Moloc and Bael. Revenant killed him last year."

"What does that have to do with me?" Realization dawned, and his eyes shot wide. "Oh, shit. My wings—"

"They belonged to Asher."

Chapter Eighteen

Numb with shock, Cipher wheeled away from Lyre. His wings—*Asher's* wings—folded and spread of their own accord, and he had the sudden desire to rip them off. No, not even a desire. A desperate *need*.

With a roar of anguish and fury, he reached over his shoulder and seized one by its bony ridge. Pain streaked through the wing and up into his neck as he tried to wrench it from his body. He was going to rip it in half. Shred it. Break it. Whatever he had to do in order to free himself of a dead angel's wings, he'd do it.

"Cipher, no!" Lyre tried to restrain him, but he threw her off like she was one of those freaky little reptile-primate things.

"How long have you known?" he yelled, the sense of betrayal hitting him harder than he figured it should.

He knew she'd been employed by Bael all this time, knew she'd do anything to get the revenge she yearned for. But this...this was sick.

"I just found out." She came toward him again.

"Bullshit!" Rage throbbed through him and he tugged harder, gritting his teeth against the agony. The other wing struck at him as if defending its partner, its claw ripping at his head.

Lyre grabbed the thing in an effort to make it stop, but it fought her as hard as it fought him. Son of a bitch! This was creepy and twisted, and what kind of sicko transplanted *wings*?

It was a stupid question given where he was. Sheoul was filled with sickos, and he was bound to become one of them if he didn't get the fuck out of here.

His struggle with the wings knocked both him and Lyre off balance, and they went down on the grass, his wings wrapping him in a tight cocoon. Increasing pressure compounded his muscles and made his bones ache as the wings tried their best to squeeze the life out of him.

"Roll onto your back." She grunted as a wing kicked out and struck her in the gut, but she managed to wrestle the thing and hold it against his shoulder.

He rolled, pinning the bastards under him. Finally, he could take a breath. Lyre stretched out next to him, panting with exertion.

"I swear to you, Cipher," she said between breaths. "Bael just told me and I went straight to you." Her hand came down on his forearm, and he found himself hoping she'd leave it there. After being so alone for so long, he craved more than a fleeting touch. More than the usual pain others doled out every time they laid hands on him. "I tried to tell you back on the island, but things were kind of crazy."

Were crazy? The crazy was still well underway. And despite his freak-out, he was grateful Lyre was here to help. She didn't have to tell him the truth, and she didn't have to rescue him from Flail's evil clutches. Hell, she'd been his sole link to sanity for months. What would his life have been like without her? His other handlers had been as depraved as Flail, bringing him food that was either too long dead or too alive, torturing him for fun, fucking with his head every chance they got.

There's no way they would have saved him from Flail or told him his wings weren't actually his.

And what the hell was up with that, anyway? Now he understood why Flail had said his wings would help him create viruses. That had been Asher's specialty. Combined with Cipher's tech skills, Bael had been counting on some serious computer-borne plagues.

As he lay there on his back, staring blankly up at the sky, he watched the programming code circling in the air far above him. He'd noticed it the moment he and Lyre had stepped outside the training facility and again here in this weird valley, but he hadn't been able to decipher it yet.

Some of it looked familiar, as if he knew the subject, if not the purpose. *Griminions*. Souls. There would be no reason to cast spells for those things unless...unless they were the spells that kept the souls of the dead inside Bael's territory and that kept *griminions* out.

"Cipher? Are you okay?"

"What? Oh, yeah." He gave a reluctant nod. "I'm just pissed. This is insane." He growled as his wings bucked beneath him. "That whack job gave me someone else's wings, and as if that wasn't bad enough, he made sure they were ensorcelled so I can't leave his realm."

"They're actually ensorcelled so you can't flash around *inside* the realm. No newbie fallen angel can leave."

He cranked his head to look at her. "So you're trapped here too?"

"Yup. I'm still on probation."

She rolled onto her side and propped herself up on one elbow, her thick ponytail draping over her shoulder and falling across her breasts. Was it wrong of him to notice that and the way her full breasts filled out her tank top?

Nah.

"Do you think part of the reason Bael gave the wings to you was to accelerate the process that turns fallen angels evil?" A breeze whipped her ponytail around until it settled in her cleavage, and he went utterly parched when she absently brushed her fingers over the thick lock of hair. "I mean, those wings are already steeped in malevolence. It should be bleeding into you."

"Maybe," he mused, refocusing on the subject and not on how much he wanted to drag his tongue along the neckline of her top. "But you'd think I'd feel more of it." He'd been shocked at how *not* evil he felt. He'd expected to be slammed with it, to have to fight it more than he had.

"I should feel more of it too." She toyed with a piece of the yellow grass, her liquid mercury gaze downcast. "I don't know what's wrong with me. For so long I felt like I should want to do evil things. I wanted evil to fill me with so much hate that I wouldn't be miserable down here."

He got that. He'd let despair get to him once or twice, making him wonder, for a split-second, how much easier life would be if he just gave in to the dark side.

Heh. Dark side. Between his Star Wars reference and Lyre's Aliens line, he figured that if they survived the next twenty-four hours they'd have to do a science-fiction marathon. With popcorn and pizza and beer. Damn, he could practically taste garlicky pepperoni and feel ice cold liquid pouring down his throat. He could invite Hawk and Journey, and—

A sinking sensation tugged at his insides. What if they hated him? What if they couldn't forgive him for giving up the list of their brothers and sisters? He didn't have to survive just the next twenty-four hours, he had to survive all his friends and the Grim Reaper.

"I think it wouldn't have been long before I got to that point." He swallowed dryly. "Knowing I'm responsible for the death of one of Azagoth's children would have fucked me up."

Still might.

"I'm so sorry." Her palm traveled up and down his arm in long, soothing strokes, and his skin tingled at the gentle touch. "I didn't know what Bael intended."

He tempered his voice, driven by curiosity, not malice. "Would it have mattered?"

"Honestly? At the time, no."

"And now?"

She closed her eyes, and he wondered if she was conscious of the way her nails dug into his skin. "Now I just want to get out of here. I don't want to be responsible for any of the catastrophic things Bael and Moloc plan to do." Her sable lashes flew up, and her eyes mirrored her sudden anger. "Now the only evil I want any part in is aimed at those assholes," she growled.

Okay, he could work with that. "Wanna do evil things together?"

"Like what?"

"Like...open Bael's realm to Azagoth." God, he hoped this wasn't a trick. He was going to lay it all out, and if she reported back to Bael, he'd be dead. But ultimately, he needed her. He couldn't do this without her. And, most significantly, he *wanted* to trust her.

"Are you serious?" she asked.

He nodded and went down the rabbit hole. "My buddies slid a code into the backdoor of Bael's security system. If I can get to my computer I can shut it down." He looked up at the sky, its eerie orange depths streaked with gray tendrils of ash. "And I think I can destroy the spell that prevents *griminions* from getting inside and that keeps souls in. If I can send a message to Hawkyn, we could coordinate everything. We can escape."

"But your wings are still enchanted. They won't let you leave his territory."

Which was why he had to lose them. "You're going to have to cut them off."

Abruptly, she sat up and stared. "Are you serious? Cipher, that'll be excruciating. And you won't be able to recharge your powers until you grow new wings. All you'll have is what's stored in your anchor bones."

All that was going to suck. Hard. But he'd gotten lots of practice being in pain, and he'd spent decades without powers while he was an Unfallen. He could do it again. As long as he had enough juice in his power battery to execute his opening salvo, his recharge could wait.

"That's why we'll need Azagoth's help. And an *aural*," he added. "I'll stab Bael myself if I get the chance. Do you know where he stores the one my opponents used in the arena?"

"He keeps it locked in the armory nearby. But it's impossible to get into. It's locked with a spell."

"Sounds right up my alley."

"Oh, yeah." She grinned. "You have a really cool gift."

He could see it coming in handy quite a bit, actually. "I just hope I don't lose it with the wings."

She nibbled her bottom lip thoughtfully. "The wings were attached to your existing bone structure. Most of the non-plague related abilities should be yours, not Asher's. But just in case, maybe you should delete the spells that keep souls in and *griminions* out now."

Made sense. Looking up at the bazillions of lines of code, he concentrated. It took longer than he would have liked to reprogram the spell and insert a timer, but after about an hour, he was finally satisfied.

He gripped Lyre's hand and squeezed. "You ready?"

"To slice off your wings?"

He suspected that they weren't going to *slice* off, all polite and easy, like a tender shaving of roast beef. But sure. "Yes."

"No."

He wished he could laugh, but the best he could do was reach across his body and snag the dagger from the sheath at her hip. "Just hurry. They're going to fight you."

Taking a quick, deep breath, he rolled onto his stomach and held onto the ground, trusting Lyre with his body, his future, and his very life.

Chapter Nineteen

Lyre had never been squeamish, and years in Sheoul had made her even less so. But sawing wings off Cipher had left her shaking with adrenaline and horror. The wet crunch of the blade sawing through bone, the resistant vibration of the knife hitting gristle, the metallic stench of his blood.

And through it all, Cipher had been silent.

She'd screamed when her own wings had been severed, and hers had been taken off neatly, with a blade meant for the task. Her wings also hadn't fought like pterodactyls caught in a net.

He knelt a few yards away, where he'd stumbled and collapsed after the second one flopped to the ground, his back bleeding, his chest heaving. She dropped the knife and ran to him.

He reached blindly for her as she went down on her knees in front of him. "Is there anything I can do?"

"No." The pain etched in his expression broke her heart. He squeezed her shoulder, using her as a brace as he straightened. "It's already getting better."

She doubted that. Taking his hand, she channeled healing waves into him. Every little bit had to help, and within moments, his color had come back a little and the flow of blood to the ground slowed to a drip.

Suddenly, he hissed and went stiff, his back arching so violently she thought his spine might snap. "Fuck...hurts..."

"I want to help, Cipher—"

He dropped forward again, catching himself on her arm. His

forehead fell to her shoulder, and he spent a dozen heartbeats like that, his labored breathing rocking his entire body.

"Thank you," he rasped.

For what? Maiming him? Hurting him? She knew she'd done what was necessary, but it didn't change the fact that she'd brutally severed a fallen angel's defining feature and the source of his power. Didn't matter that they weren't his. He felt it as if they were.

"Shh," she murmured. "Rest. Heal."

Without his wings, the healing process would take longer, but already the edges of his wounds were less ragged and starting to seal up, and his skin had lost the ashen tone.

He relaxed against her, the tension in his big frame draining with every passing minute.

Gently, she held him, stroking his damp hair until he looked up at her, his tormented gaze locking onto hers. "I'm sorry."

Her mouth fell open with shock. "Are you kidding? For what?"

"For making you do this." He reached up, his hand trembling as he cupped her cheek. "It couldn't have been easy."

No, it hadn't been. But she'd definitely been on the less horrible end of the blade, and it amazed her, humbled her, that his concern wasn't for himself, but for her. What a magnificent male he was.

The last of her walls crumbled, and she leaned into his touch, selfishly taking comfort from him when she was the one who should be comforting him. His mouth was just inches from hers, his breath fanning her lips, and she found herself wanting even more from him.

"Lyre?" His deep voice was soft, and yet, it hung in the air as a resonant echo.

"Yes?" she whispered.

"If we don't make it out of here alive, I don't want the last thing we did to be...this."

She melted. All her emotions melted, just puddled in the lower chambers of her heart at his tender words.

"What are you saying?" she whispered back, even though she knew.

She hoped. This might not be the ideal place, but it was the perfect time. Nothing in her life had been under her control for years. She'd basically signed everything over to Bael, including her virginity, apparently.

Well, screw that. She'd just thrown in with Cipher, and if they failed in their attempt at escape, she'd either die or end up in Bael's bed. She didn't want to do either of those things without having experienced the kind of passion Cipher promised.

His mouth closed on hers, and as if he'd lit a fuse, her body sparked to life. Sizzling, fiery life, brought back from the cold, dead ashes of her past.

She opened to him, and his tongue slid between her lips and stroked hers, deepening the kiss as he pushed her onto her back. He wasn't rough, but he wasn't gentle, either. There was a desperate urgency to the way he tore open first her pants and then his, and as he kissed his way down her jaw and along her throat, tiny, hot nibbles left her moaning for more.

He gave her exactly that, making love to her with his mouth all the way to the top of her breasts, where he swept his tongue along the edge of her neckline.

"That's so sexy," she whispered, arching to help him shove her bra-lined tank up.

"No," he said, as he gazed at her bare breasts. "This is."

Lowering his head, he opened his mouth over her breast and sucked gently, sending a series of erotic tingles spiraling through her. His tongue was magic, stroking and licking each breast as his hands shoved her pants down her legs.

Eagerly she helped him, clawing at the stupid cargoes and then kicking at them when they tangled around her ankles. Finally, she flung them aside and welcomed Cipher between her thighs.

His hands were everywhere, tickling her ribs, stroking the sensitive skin at her hipbones, and delving lower to her swollen sex. She rolled her hips to meet his touch as she wrapped her arms around him. Her hands slid through slick smears of blood, and when she cried out in sorrow that she might be hurting him, he shifted and grasped her wrist, holding it at his back.

"No," he breathed against her collarbone. "Your touch only makes it better."

Oh, damn. He was so sweet, so strong, so out of place in this awful world. She fell for him right then and there, her pledge to remain emotionally detached gone up in the flames he was stoking in her as he slipped a finger between her folds.

She nearly sobbed with emotion and pleasure as he caressed her, his fingertip circling her clit with alternating measures of pressure, and adding feather light flicks at the tip and a few heartbeats of intense, steady pressure at the base.

She couldn't bear it, the way he manipulated her body with the same nimble precision he used with a keyboard. Her climax hit her so hard she couldn't breathe, could barely even gasp for air as ripples of ecstasy spread all the way to her toes and scalp.

"That's it," he murmured. "Keep coming."

Keep coming? Her body was all over that command, and another explosion rocked her.

"Again," he whispered, and damn if she didn't ride his hand to another orgasm.

"What are you doing to me?" she cried out as she peaked, because whatever it was, he could keep doing it.

His hot breath fanned her neck as he shifted, positioning himself at her entrance. "Programming you." His deep voice rumbled with masculine need. "This is how you'll always respond to me."

Oh...yes.

Hooking her ankles around his thighs, she arched into him, moaning at the sensation of his broad head pushing past the tight ring of her core. The stretching sensation was bearable; the wait was not.

Panting with exertion and anticipation, she managed a breathless, "Are you saying you hacked my network?"

He looked down at her, his blue eyes glowing with intensity, a hint of a smile on his lips. "You had a strong password, but I haven't met one yet that I can't crack."

His hips rolled as he eased inside her. Pain and pleasure mingled, and this was so much more than she could have hoped for. She'd always regretted that she and Dailon had never consummated their relationship, but now she knew why they hadn't. As an angel she'd always believed that everything happened for a reason, and that there was always a plan.

But she'd lost that faith to bitterness in recent years. Maybe this was a sign that she'd been right all along, because she knew, without a doubt, that this was the moment an intimate connection was needed.

An intimate connection that reminded her to live, to love, to fight for life.

Hers, *and* his.

* * * *

This was the best sex Cipher had ever had, and he hadn't even come yet.

Holy hell, Lyre was tight, her slick channel barely accommodating him, squeezing so hard he didn't even have to move. She was doing more than enough to make him clench his teeth and hope for control.

That lasted about two seconds.

With a groan of shame, he rocked against her, sliding in and out in a slow, easy rhythm that had her making soft, sexy sounds as she clenched around him. She was close again, so responsive to his touch and his body, and shit, he needed to play with that. A lot. When they got out of here, he was going to find every erogenous zone and he was going to make her come until they both passed out.

"Cipher, I-I'm..." Her sexed-up voice put him over the top as she shouted in release.

He let himself go, lunging into her and sliding her backward in the grass with the force of his thrusts. Surging, his hips driving home as if he needed to claim her so deeply she'd always feel him, he came hard, the ecstasy reaching every part of his body.

It didn't stop, and at the height of it, his wing anchors, raw and exposed to the elements, rolled into the position they would have taken for an angel's embrace, the cocoon of wings around an angel and his partner.

Ah, damn, he'd gone all in with Lyre, hadn't he?

He could hear Hawkyn now, all, "Cipher, the consummate playboy, the jackass who got my Memitim sentence extended with his uncontrollable need to nail everything that moved, finally got his angel ass plucked."

Or Hawkyn would kill him and never have to the chance to call him "plucked." Such stupid terms the young punk Memitim were using these days.

The last ripples of pleasure wrung him out, leaving him heaving above Lyre, his arms trembling with the strain of holding himself up as she undulated through her waning climax. Her sixth, maybe? He wasn't sure, but he loved watching her expression and the way her glistening lips parted with each delicate cry.

Finally, she went limp, her fingers caressing his tender back as she pulled him down on top of her.

"Wow." Turning her head, she kissed his cheek as he lay at the curve of her shoulder. "That wasn't what I expected."

"Better or worse?" If she said worse, he was never telling Hawkyn this story.

She chuckled. "Better. Way, way better."

Okay, somehow that answer wasn't any more desirable. "Ah...what were you expecting?"

"More pain, I guess."

He pushed himself up on one elbow, ignoring the stabbing discomfort where his wings used to be.

"Did you *want* pain?" He really wasn't into that, but he figured he could get some tips from Journey. That guy liked his whips and chains and nipple clamps. "And why were you expecting it? Do I scream Dom, or what?"

Her half-lidded, satiated smile stroked his masculine pride. Stroked his cock too, and it stirred. How, he had no idea. His muscles were basically soup right now.

"No, I don't think I'm into pain, and no, you don't scream Dom." She wriggled onto her side, and he slid from her warm body, to his acute disappointment. "It was my first time. I just thought it would be less enjoyable. But it was *really* enjoyable."

First time? He stared, unsure how to respond. Or how to feel. She'd given him something she'd held on to for over a century. Something she'd managed to safeguard while living in Sheoul, where innocence and purity were ultra-rare commodities to be selectively ruined in the most useful or evil way imaginable.

Finally, he managed a lame, "Why me? Why now?"

"It had to be you." She reached over and twined her fingers with his. "I know, because I was ready to have sex with you in your cell and later in my flat."

She averted her gaze, and he hated it, reached out and tilted her chin up so their eyes met. "Why now?" he repeated. "Tell me, angel."

Strength and resolve swam in her liquid mercury eyes. "It's because I needed it. If I'm going to fight, I need a reason to win."

He inhaled deeply, thankful that she'd been assigned as his handler. Thankful for *her*. What she lacked in angelic ability she more than made up for with her brains, her fiercely protective nature, and her determination.

"We'll win." Reluctantly, he grabbed her pants and slid them over her feet, enjoying the intimacy of helping her dress. That small act was somehow even more personal than sex. "If Azagoth helps us escape, we can't lose."

"You think he'll help after—" She broke off, biting her lip.

"After I betrayed him and got one of his kids killed?" He buttoned his own jeans as she buttoned hers. "He won't be *helping* me. He'll be *using* me to kill Bael." And then he'd probably kill Cipher.

Small details.

He suppressed a groan at the ache in his back as he stood and held out a hand to her. "You ready?"

Taking his hand, Lyre nodded. "Whatever happens...thank you."

"For what?" Needing an excuse to touch her, he tucked her tank top into her pants, letting his fingers linger on her firm rear. "I'm probably going to get you killed."

"For reminding me that there's more to live for than revenge." She smiled wanly. "The downside is that now dying would suck."

Pretty much. Holding his breath, he looked up at the sky, afraid of what he'd see.

Or *wouldn't* see.

Relief nearly knocked him to his knees. There, in the gray-streaked orange sky, were the transparent characters that made up the spell codes. He didn't want to waste the power remaining in the stems of his wings since he had no way to recharge now, but just a teeny bit couldn't hurt. He opened himself to a trickle of power and zapped a character out of existence before replacing it a heartbeat later.

Fucking awesome. It was *his* power, not Asher's.

Now he just had to survive long enough to use it.

Chapter Twenty

A dull pain throbbed in Cipher's wing anchors as he and Lyre slipped inside the room where his poor laptop sat, all cold and alone. But his body felt revitalized, his mind refreshed.

Amazing what sex can do for a guy, huh?

It wasn't just the sex that had him hopped up on positive energy. Ridding himself of the heavy taint of malevolence that had come with Asher's wings had been like a weight off his shoulders. Literally.

He remembered how bereft he'd felt after losing his heavenly wings, how depressed and physically ill he'd been. But if losing his heavenly wings had dragged him down, losing the transplanted evil ones had filled him with power that had nothing to do with angelic energy.

He was, once again, his own master.

They'd also successfully gotten in and out of Bael's armory with clean pants and a tee he'd pilfered from a guard he'd knocked out, as well as with a weapon protected by a nasty spell that would have turned them both inside out if he hadn't been able to break it.

But beneath the bliss was a thread of fear. Not for his life, but fear for Lyre. And the world. If they didn't stop Bael, the crazy motherfucker was going to trash human life, Heavenly life, and Azagoth's entire world. And once Satan was free, the trash pile was going to get even bigger.

That guy had a score to settle.

"Can you really bring down his security systems?" Lyre asked. "Even with your powers diminished?"

"Yup." He fired up his baby. "It's all about the computer. No magic involved."

She paced around the room, her nerves showing with every quick step, every nibble on her nails. "How long will it be before the soul barrier spells are down?"

He checked the clock on the computer. "If I didn't screw anything up, we have about ten minutes."

"Is that enough time to bring down his security systems?"

He tapped his way into Bael's security backdoor and looked for the trigger Journey had installed. "It should be."

"Should be?" Her fingers went absently to the *aural* tucked inside her waistband, covered by her shirt. It was still visible, but it was more likely to be mistaken as a dagger than recognized as a rare, ancient angel-killing stake. "Bael is going to know the moment the protective spells are gone, and he's going to know who did it."

"I know." There was Journey's backdoor. All Cipher had to do was flip a virtual switch, and every bit of Bael's tech would fail. If Journey himself had written the program, it would take Bael's best technicians hours, if not days, to get it up and running again. The Memitim was that good.

"Can Bael repair the spells?"

"I fucked them up pretty bad. If he tries to use the same spells again, they'll fail. Eventually his sorcerers will try new formulas, but I bought us some time to escape." He looked over at her. "Your inability to flash out of Bael's realm is tied to the spell barriers, right?" At her nod, he continued. "Then all you have to do is flash us out of here once they're down."

She snorted. "First we have to make it out of the building and across the drawbridge. No one can flash in or out of his castle or the surrounding grounds, and you know he's going to lock everything down."

Which was why they'd have to run really, really fast. While being completely inconspicuous.

"We just have to trust that Azagoth will come through," he said, and she gave a skeptical snort.

"I still don't understand how you can trust any of those people."

"Not everyone is out to hurt you, Lyre," he said softly.

He popped open his message app and shot Hawkyn a note. Glanced at the computer clock. The spells should break outside in 3...2...1.

"It's time."

He flipped the switch.

* * * *

"Father!"

Hawkyn ignored Zhubaal's warnings that Azagoth was not only busy but also not in the best of moods, and he burst into Azagoth's office.

"I got a message from Cipher," Hawkyn said breathlessly. "He's brought down Bael's security system and the soul barrier."

Azagoth turned away from the *griminion* he'd been speaking to. "So I've been informed." He'd probably felt the soul barrier's collapse himself.

"So what are we going to do? Cipher needs help, and none of us can enter that part of Sheoul." It was damned inconvenient, too. There were a lot of places inside Sheoul where angels couldn't—or wouldn't—go. Most parts of Sheoul, in fact. "Whatever it is, we need to hurry. Bael will have everything up and running again soon."

And then Cipher, if he couldn't escape in time, would die.

"I'll take care of it." Azagoth gestured to the little robed *griminion*, and the critter skittered away.

"Take care of what?" It could be dangerous to question the Grim Reaper, but Hawkyn had found that if he didn't nail down specifics, Azagoth found loopholes. Azagoth could find a loophole in a straight steel rod.

"Bael." Azagoth's voice dipped low, daring Hawkyn to ask another question.

Hawkyn dared. This was too important not to. "What about Cipher?"

"I'll take care of him too."

Azagoth's tone was chilling, and Hawkyn growled. "I want him back alive. Not barely alive. Not mostly alive. Alive and *well*. With a physical body."

Crimson streaks flared in Azagoth's black eyes as his anger and malevolence escalated. "*He killed my daughter.*"

"No, he didn't." Hawkyn dug his phone out of his pocket. "Just before Hawkyn's message, I got word from the Memitim Council. Amelia was Primori."

"What?" Azagoth's shock morphed instantly into doubt and anger. "How can any of my children be Primori?" he snapped. "They're Memitim. They can't be both."

Hawkyn had been as stunned by the news as Azagoth was. As far as he knew, no Memitim had also held the protected status of Primori.

"I don't know, but the Council confirmed it. Amelia had a Memitim guardian from the moment of her birth. He was taken off the job just hours before she was killed." When Azagoth just stood there, his fury congealing in his eyes, Hawkyn beat him over the head with the obvious. "Father, she was *meant* to die."

And what *that* meant was anyone's guess.

With a hiss, Azagoth turned toward the entrance to the Inner Sanctum, but Hawkyn grabbed his arm.

"*Please*, Father. He's my best friend." He tempered his tone, not caring if he sounded like he was begging. Because that's what he was doing. "Cipher's been through a lot with me. He's an honorable male."

Azagoth shook off his touch but didn't turn around. When he spoke, he spoke to the wall. "And if becoming a True Fallen has changed that?"

Hawkyn swallowed, knowing the correct answer but not wanting to say it. Hell, he didn't even want to think it. But if he wanted his father to give Cipher even half a chance, he had to.

"If Cipher has turned evil," he said, "I'll put him down myself."

Chapter Twenty-One

Alarms blared as Cipher and Lyre crept through the ice hallways and narrow, winding stairwells of Bael's castle. Armored Ramreel guards charged toward duty stations, exits, and Bael's residence, their crude axes and spiked maces clutched tight in their meaty fists. They weren't specifically searching for Cipher yet, but it wouldn't be long before Bael filtered through the chaos and realized that only Cipher could have been responsible for the failure of not only the security system, but the downing of the soul barrier as well.

"This way." Lyre tugged him down a corridor lit by flickering torch sconces that cast snarling, demonic faces in shadow. "There's a side door. We can take the staircase into the outer dungeons."

"Dungeons?" He glanced over his shoulder at a Ramreel that had followed them into the passage. Maybe it was coincidence. "Isn't that what we're trying to avoid?"

"There's a tunnel from there that leads into the Bowel Mountains. Once we're out, if the barrier is still down, I can flash us out of Bael's territory. If the barrier is up again, we'll still be ahead of his troops, and I know where we can access a Harrowgate that'll get us into the human realm."

A horde of several species of demons rounded the corner ahead, the leader's dozens of eyes lighting up when he saw them.

No coincidence there.

"Shit!" She pulled him down another hallway. "Plan B."

"What's Plan B?"

"Run fast."

He hated that plan. They took off at a dead run, the demons closing the distance behind them way too quickly.

"Hurry!" he shouted, putting on a burst of speed as the sound of snapping teeth rang out so close to his head he felt hot breath on the back of his neck.

"Out the front," she yelled. "We can lose them in the chaos."

Ahead, the giant double doors were open. Beyond the doorway in the courtyard, confused demons milled about beneath decorative corpses swinging overheard.

Cipher risked a glance behind him and instantly regretted his mistake. The number of pursuing guards had doubled.

He summoned the precious remains of his power, holding it at his fingertips and ready to strike. He was weaker without the wings, but even now he could feel the increase in control. A tradeoff, but really, in a fight it might be better to have uncontrolled strength than controlled crumbs of power.

This was not going to be a piece of cake.

But if they made it out of this alive, he was going to ask Suzanne to make one to celebrate.

They burst outside, jumping into the midst of hundreds of beings who clearly had no idea what was happening but wanted to be in the middle of the action.

Demons were stupid.

"There!" Lyre pointed toward the bridge that spanned the lava moat. "Once we're across, I can flash us out of here."

Okay. This might work. Hope trickled through him.

And then he looked up and jerked to a stop. "Oh, shit," he breathed. *Oh, fuck.*

"What is it?"

"The spells. They're not down. Azagoth can't get help in here and we can't get out—"

A massive explosion rocked the ground ahead. The bridge collapsed as giant boulders of rock and ice spewed into the air and cratered all around them, crushing demons, carts, and the stands where they sold their wares.

With shrieks of terror and pain all around, Cipher knocked Lyre to the ground, covering her with his body as debris rained down. Basketball-sized chunks pummeled his back and legs, but he'd survive.

Unlike that poor bastard with his hooves sticking out under a Volkswagen-sized block of ice, his blood spreading in a pool beneath him.

"*I will slaughter you where you stand!*"

Bael's voice, sounding way too close, froze the blood in Cipher's veins. He leaped to his feet, heart pounding and pushing that frozen blood like slush that left him feeling like shit was in slow motion.

A crack of thunder shattered his eardrums a split-second before a lightning strike sizzled through him, paralyzing him where he stood. Agony became everything, his feelings, his thoughts, his vision. Because apparently, you could *see* pain. It was red and shiny and twisted as fuck.

Distantly, he heard Lyre's shouts for mercy. Not mercy for her. Mercy for him.

"Stop," she yelled. "I'll do anything!"

"Yes," Bael hissed. "You will."

No! Cipher inhaled, coughing on blood as he staggered forward blindly, his only goal to reach Bael and choke the life out of him with his bare hands.

He heard a grunt, a thud, and suddenly the electrocution stopped. His ears rang and white spots floated in his vision, but the pain died to a dull roar, and as his eyes focused, he saw why.

Lyre had tackled Bael.

But she'd paid for it, was now trying to pick herself up off the ground, blood pouring from her nose and ears. Bael laughed as he punched down, hitting her in the back of the neck and dropping her as if she'd been hit with a bolt.

His fist tangled in her hair, and he brutally wrenched her head up, putting his mouth to her ear. Cipher couldn't hear what he was saying, but he heard Lyre's cry of terror.

"Bastard!" Cipher roared in fury and released the first weapon that came to mind, a barrage of voracious summoned demon locusts that swarmed Bael in a whirlwind of teeth.

Bael howled in pain as he was cut to ribbons, giving Lyre a chance to push to her feet.

"Come on!" Cipher held out his hand to her. "Hurry!"

She started toward him, but suddenly, the locusts fell dead. Son of a bitch! The locust swarm had drained his power by half, and Bael had circumvented it as if the locusts had been no more than a nuisance.

Bael, his ire taking on a life of its own, transformed, his body tripling in size, his skin hardening into black armor, his face taking on nightmarish, oversized features and teeth the size of Cipher's fingers.

They couldn't score a freaking break.

With the very last of his power, he blasted Bael with his ice melt weapon, encasing the bastard from head to toe. "Lyre, run!"

"No!" She sprinted toward him, and he wanted to scream at the futility of it. She couldn't help him. She'd just die with him.

"Go!"

A detonation of ice sent piercing shards into the demons who had gathered to watch, and by some miracle both he and Lyre had escaped unscathed. Some of the demons dropped dead while others hit the ground and thrashed in pain. Still others ran.

Bael, completely ice-free, roared in fury and blasted Cipher and Lyre with some sort of weapon that sliced a million tiny cuts into the skin and peeled it away.

Agony became the very air Cipher breathed, and through his own shouts of misery, Lyre's screams punched through, flaying his insides as well.

"You're going to die," Bael shouted above the thunder that rolled in from the blood-red storm clouds above. "You're going to die, and then I'm going to feed your souls to my Orphmage while I dine on your flesh." The fallen angel sauntered toward him. "But not before you get to watch what Moloc and I do to your precious Lyre."

No. Please no...

Darkness started to fall. Maybe not in the realm, but in Cipher's head. He couldn't lift his arms, his legs, his head. Hell, he could barely open his eyes.

He saw Lyre writhing on the ground, and his heart, already riddled with wounds, bled. Tortured by the sight, he put all of his strength into reaching for her. If he could just touch her...

A demon shrieked and ran between them, nearly stepping on his arm. Then another. All around, terrified wails rose up. Suddenly, Bael spun around, his attention and restraining powers no longer focused on Cipher and Lyre.

What the hell?

Groaning, Cipher glanced at the sky. The spells...the spells had broken!

Something, or some *things*, were attacking the demons, and for the first time, Bael looked afraid.

"Lyre," he croaked as he pushed himself to his hands and knees on shaky limbs.

She looked over at him. Looked at Bael.

And then she looked back at him again, determination mirrored in her glittering eyes. What was she going to do?

"Lyre?"

She vaporized into a puff of smoke, and before he could even blink, she shot into Bael's nostrils. His eyes popped wide and he grabbed his throat, choking and gagging.

And Lyre, that wily little angel, had left the *aural* on the ground.

Cipher staggered to his feet. His legs were rubber and his steps leaden, but he managed to palm the *aural* and somehow make it to where Bael was struggling to exorcise Lyre.

Clutching his throat, Bael wheeled around to face Cipher, the hatred in his expression making his face bulge grotesquely. He lifted a clawed hand, shocks of electricity sparking between his fingers, and Cipher knew that this next blow would kill him.

There was no time left.

He lunged, slamming the *aural* into Bael's chest.

And nothing happened. The weapon slid uselessly off his armor.

Fuck!

Still coughing, Bael grinned, raised his hand once more.

Then, from out of nowhere, a transparent gray, shapeless form wrapped around Bael, its eyes empty, its mouth screaming silently.

Bael's scream was *not* silent.

One of Azagoth's souls. Way to go, Hawkyn!

Lyre's vapor form ejected from between Bael's lips as the fallen angel returned to his original, angel-sized body. He writhed in misery as the soul spun around him, doing whatever it was souls did.

But no, that soul wasn't going to claim this kill.

This kill belonged to Cipher.

With a battle cry soaked in vengeance, Cipher buried the *aural* in Bael's heart. This time the weapon slammed home.

Bael gasped as his body shuddered and convulsed, smoke rising from the cracks forming in his skin. The sizzle of burning flesh accompanied his death cries, and the evil inside Cipher was transfixed by it all.

Finally, as Lyre wrapped herself around Cipher and held him tight, the fucker collapsed.

Bael was dead. The monster who had terrorized this region of Sheoul for eons was gone.

Somehow, they'd survived this, but Cipher still had one more monster to face, and his name was Azagoth.

Chapter Twenty-Two

Azagoth hated waiting.

People were always amazed by his patience, but they only saw what he wanted them to see. His exterior was very much different than his interior.

Inside was a high-strung, restless beast that didn't like to wait for things like vengeance. Or pleasure.

At least now that Lilliana was home, it didn't have to wait for the latter. Her presence had soothed the monster until now, as he waited for news coming out of Sheoul. He'd sent hundreds of souls to destroy Bael, and with any luck, Moloc would be with his brother as well.

But so far his *griminions* hadn't brought him their souls. They'd delivered dozens of other souls they'd reaped from Bael's realm, but not the ones Azagoth wanted.

This was taking too long.

A massive power surge forced the hair on Azagoth's neck to stand up, and before he could even blink, another, equally powerful wave of energy slammed into him.

Fuck.

Reaver and Revenant had just popped in for a visit, and Azagoth had no doubt that this wasn't going to be a friendly one.

Which meant that he was going to meet them in the place of his choosing, the place that gave him a strategic advantage.

He threw open his office door just as Zhubaal skidded to a stop in front of it. "My lord—"

"I know. Send them to the Inner Sanctum."

Z jerked. "M-my lord?"

"Do it. And send someone to keep Lilliana occupied. I don't want her near Reaver or Revenant." He doubted either male would harm Lilliana, but he wouldn't put it past them to use her in some way if they had to.

"Yes, sir."

Quickly, he went through the passage to the Inner Sanctum, and within moments of stepping across the threshold, Hades materialized.

"Hey, boss man," Hades said, his blue Mohawk cut close to his head today. "Who are you here to torture?"

"I'm not torturing anyone. We're expecting guests, and we only have about sixty seconds to prepare."

"Guests?"

"Reaver and Revenant."

Hades's eyes shot wide open. "But won't their presence weaken the veil between Sheoul and Sheoul-gra?"

"I'm counting on it," Azagoth said. "They know they can't destroy me here without blowing out the barriers and releasing millions of demon souls."

There was no way either angel would risk that. The resulting chaos would spread quickly, affecting not just the demon realm, but the human one as well. They wouldn't stay long, either, knowing that their mere presence would burn holes through the veil like acid.

Hades nodded. "Understood. I'll put my repair crew on standby."

"No." Azagoth glanced over at the portal the angels would be coming through at any moment. "I don't want you to fix any damage their presence causes."

"The fuck you say?" If Hades had ever been more stunned by anything, Azagoth wasn't aware of it. He cleared his throat and added a hasty, "My lord?"

Not in the mood to either explain his command or be questioned about it, he snapped, "Go. They'll be here in a moment."

Hades popped his wings and lifted off just as Reaver and Revenant stepped out of the portal.

Reaver stalked toward him like a bull, his expression shadowed with fury, his pristine white and gold wings flared high above gleaming crimson and gold armor. Revenant flanked him, his black and silver wings folded tamely against the backplate of his light-absorbing ebony armor, but there was nothing tame about his bared fangs. Both angels were prepped for battle, and Azagoth flooded his body with power in response.

"I warned you not to release souls." Reaver's voice, singing with strength, vibrated the very air. "I warned you not to kill Bael."

Guilty as charged on point A. But point B was a bust. Not for lack of trying though. His disappointment in not being brought Bael's soul was almost crushing.

"Chill the fuck out, boys," Azagoth said. "If Bael was dead, his soul would have come to me, and I'd be dissecting it right now."

Sure, it was possible that another incredibly powerful demon or fallen angel had destroyed or devoured his soul, but the odds of that were so low as to be preposterous.

Reaver looked out over the stark terrain of what was basically the antechamber to the rest of the Inner Sanctum, and Azagoth wondered if he noticed the demons in the distance, slowly moving toward them, drawn by the power emanating from the two angels.

"You're wrong." Reaver turned back to Azagoth. "*Griminions* couldn't have harvested his soul. He and his brother Moloc were...aberrations."

Azagoth scoffed. "What do you mean, aberrations?"

"They're twins," Reaver said. "But they are one."

Revenant's head cranked around to stare at his brother. "Say what?"

"They share a soul," Reaver explained. "To kill one of them means reuniting their two halves and making the remaining 'brother' whole. And much, much stronger."

Well, wasn't that interesting. Azagoth *had* succeeded in killing Bael's physical body. Unfortunately, the fucker was still alive inside another body, and even stronger than before.

Fan-fucking-tastic.

"You couldn't have shared that information sooner?" he gritted out.

Revenant jabbed Reaver in the shoulder. "No shit."

Reaver glared at them both. "I didn't know either, assholes. I just found out a few hours ago when I looked them up in the Akashic Library."

Man, Azagoth missed the Heavenly library that contained details about every human, every event, every *thing* in the history of the universe.

"So?" Revenant crossed his arms over his chest, his spiked gauntlets clanking against his armor. "What's their story?"

Azagoth was curious as well. Not because he gave a shit, but because information was a weapon.

"Apparently," Reaver began, "their split-soul is why they were banished from Heaven as the youngest angels in history. According to the texts, they were devoid of empathy, and they delighted in hurting others. Humans, animals, other angels. They were going to be executed, but Moloc escaped. Bael couldn't be executed for fear of reuniting the souls, so the archangels cut off his wings and kicked him out. Moloc performed a ceremony and his own wingectomy, and he fell too. Both joined up with Satan, and here we are."

Minor setback. Azagoth just had to kill Moloc now. MolocBael? BaelMoloc? Whatever. Minor. Fucking. Setback.

So why didn't it feel so minor? Alarm bells were ringing hard on this.

"Listen to me, Azagoth," Reaver said. "I know you killed Bael. You fucked up. Don't do it again. Don't kill Moloc."

"Or what?"

"Or you'll cease to exist."

Klaxons joined the alarm bells, and an entire symphony of warnings vibrated his body now. "You're threatening me?"

"No, Azagoth, I'm telling you." Reaver's voice went low, ominous, his wings quivering with the force of it. "If you kill him, all that you know, all that you are...will be destroyed."

Sudden fury seared Azagoth's veins, hot and potent. "Do you not understand what Bael and Moloc want? They want Satan freed and Revenant deposed, and they're killing my family to make it happen!" He rounded on Revenant. "Why can't you do anything about this? You're the fucking King of Hell. Surely you're not going sit back and lose your throne to an insurrection."

"Oh, I have plans for Moloc," Revenant drawled. "I'm more concerned about you."

"Isn't that sweet."

Revenant smirked. "Not that kind of concerned."

Of course not. Why would he give a shit about Azagoth's family? "You'd better *get* concerned," Azagoth growled. "Or the entire underworld is going to read your inaction as cowardice."

Revenant bared his fangs, his eyes went nightmare, and before Azagoth could even blink, the guy was in his face. "Call me a coward again."

"Step off, asshole," Azagoth warned. "This is my fucking realm, and you have no power here."

A flash of light nearly blinded him as Revenant lit up like a supernova, proving just how wrong Azagoth was.

"I can *melt* you if I want to, soul boy."

An invisible force knocked Azagoth into a mausoleum, triggering his temper and his inner demon. He unfurled into his beast, his horns and great wings reaching skyward.

"*How dare you.*" His voice, warped by his fury and his form, made the very ground shift under their feet. "How dare you attack me inside my realm."

Revenant hissed and shook off Reaver's restraining hand. "You attacked my realm by sending souls to do your bidding in violation of the treaty. What's your next move? Freeing Satan?"

"Never," he snarled, his shock at the very idea bringing his fury down a notch.

Revenant's wings spread wide, the bony claws at the tips clenching as if they wanted to shred Azagoth like pulled pork. "Are you sure?"

Was he sure? Satan had blackmailed Azagoth for eons, threatening his realm and his children if Azagoth refused to reincarnate the souls Satan wanted. He'd slaughtered *griminions*. He'd demanded loyalty Azagoth refused to give, and always it was one of Azagoth's children who paid.

So fuck Revenant and the hell stallion he rode in on. "Do not question my hatred for Satan," Azagoth roared.

Blood boiling, he attacked. He could have used any of a thousand weapons at his disposal, but what he wanted was to feel flesh rending between his teeth and blood streaming between his claws.

Revenant hit him head on. The shockwave of the impact blew structures apart for as far as Azagoth could see in the brief glimpse he got before Revenant's fist pounded his face and broke every bone in his head.

The pain as his skull knitted itself back together only pissed him off more, and he clamped down on Rev's throat in a bite that crushed the angel's windpipe and spine. Blood poured down Azagoth's throat, hot and powerful, and then Reaver wrenched them apart, blasting them both a hundred yards in opposite directions.

"*Enough!*"

Suddenly, Azagoth found himself hanging in the air at the end of Reaver's fingers. Revenant was at Reaver's other hand, clutching his mangled throat. Good. Fucker. Inside the Inner Sanctum, he wasn't healing as quickly as he should have.

Reaver dropped his brother to the ground. "Are we done?"

"He started it," Revenant rasped.

Shaking his head in exasperation, Reaver turned to Azagoth and dropped him next. "How can we know you won't conspire with someone to release Satan?"

Baring his teeth, he put everything he had into what he was about to say. He felt this to the depths of his soul and in the blood that ran in his veins.

"I. Will. Die. First."

Silence stretched as the stench of char swirled around them. Then, finally, Reaver nodded. "Okay. Give Lilliana my best. And congratulations on becoming a father again."

"Ditto," Revenant rasped. "Asshole."

Azagoth inclined his head and watched the brothers leave before surveying the damage to the Inner Sanctum. As he'd noted earlier, everything all around had been flattened and scorched. A few souls might have been disintegrated, but he didn't care. What he cared about was the fact that a small section of the barrier between the Inner Sanctum and Sheoul had weakened. Just a single, tiny, hairline crack in the veil that no one else but Hades would be able to see.

Smiling, he brushed himself off and whistled a jaunty tune as he headed toward the portal back to Sheoul-gra. But when he stepped into his office, he checked up hard.

Lilliana was sitting there in his chair, her expression drawn, one hand clutching a sweating glass of ice tea.

"What is it?" He rushed to her. "What's wrong?"

"I don't know," she said softly. "You tell me."

"Nothing is going on."

She looked at him like he was a dumbass. "I'm not a fool. You're covered in blood, your horns are out, and something rocked Sheoul-gra hard enough to topple statues and break dishes just minutes after Reaver and Revenant arrived. So don't bullshit me." She came to her feet, and when he reached to help her, she swatted his hand away. "You released souls to kill Bael, and they found out, didn't they?"

Azagoth had always kept his work and his home life separate. He'd never wanted Lilliana to be exposed to the ugly part of his job...or the ugly part of himself. He didn't want her to see how the soul sausage was made, when it came down to it.

"I don't want you to worry, Lilli. You've got enough to deal with as it is."

"Don't," she warned. "Don't shut me out. Never again. You swore."

He wanted to deny that he was shutting her out. And if he was, he wanted to assure her that he was doing it for her own good. But shutting her out was part of what had led to her leaving him in the first place. He'd held her hostage emotionally, not giving her that bit of him that she craved. And then when he had expressed emotion, it was anger. Always anger.

He'd promised he'd do better. It was time to fulfill that promise.

"You're right." He inhaled softly. "Bael's dead, and the Wonder Twins know about it. But they're the least of my concerns. Moloc's still alive, and he's more powerful than ever. He's going to come after me with everything he's got."

"That's why you've put a rush on bringing in the last of your human-realm children, isn't it? To get them out of the way."

He nodded. "And it's why you always have a guard. Moloc will stop at nothing to get what he wants from me."

Earlier, Lilliana had mentioned that the hellhound she'd befriended on Ares's island might be joining them, and the mutt was welcome. He wasn't fond of the beasts, but they were fiercely loyal, and no one would fuck with Lilliana with one at her side.

"Why does Moloc need you so badly?" Lilliana asked.

He reached for his favorite bottle of rum. "Because I have the key to Satan's prison."

"The key?" She lost color in her face and sank back into the chair. "Satan is in Sheoul-gra?"

"Yes and no." He abandoned the bottle and moved to her. He needed her more than the alcohol anyway. "When Revenant and Reaver trapped Satan, they created an inter-dimensional prison using the same basic frequency as the Inner Sanctum. Satan's cell is both inside Sheoul-gra and not inside it. I, alone, can access it." Leaning against the desk, he rethought that. "Well, Reaver and Revenant can too, but only if they can find it."

Lilliana looked down at her belly. "I don't like this, Azagoth."

Which was why he hadn't wanted to tell her about any of it. He'd wanted all the stress, all the ugliness, on his shoulders. Not hers. But no matter what, he'd protect her, and he'd keep her safe, no matter what it took.

"I don't either, Lilli," he said, dipping his head to give her a kiss that was more than affection. It was a promise. "But I won't let anything happen to you or our child."

Stepping back, he pulled a gold-tipped white feather from the sleeve of his right arm, and a silver-tipped black feather from the left and laid them on the desktop. Neither Reaver nor Revenant had noticed when he'd lifted them from their wings.

Lilliana reached for them, her slender fingers skimming over the delicate glitter. "What are these? I mean, obviously they're feathers, but what for?"

"Insurance," he said grimly. "They're insurance."

Chapter Twenty-Three

Cipher held Lyre's hand as they stood near the portal that would get them into Sheoul-gra. Well, it would if they had permission. Apparently Azagoth had recently sealed it after the death of one of his children.

"Can you see it?" Lyre asked, referring to the spell that kept the entrance closed.

"Yup."

"Having second thoughts?"

"What, about breaking a spell that the Grim Reaper put in place to protect his realm?" He snorted. "Nah."

She squeezed his hand reassuringly, well aware that he was having second thoughts. Third thoughts. Fourth thoughts.

There were a whole lot of thoughts going through his head right now.

"We don't have to do this," she said. "We could disappear somewhere. Live away from everyone else." She shrugged one battered shoulder, still bruised and bloodied from the battle. Her major wounds had healed already, the fractured bones and lacerations, but without wings his damage was taking far longer. "I heard Pestilence lived in a cave for centuries. So, you know, there's that."

He knew she was kidding about the cave—probably—but no matter what, life as a fugitive from Azagoth's wrath and his friends' scorn wouldn't work for him. He'd always been an *act first, ask forgiveness later* type of guy, but he did always ask forgiveness.

"I can't run, Lyre." Both literally and figuratively. He was pretty sure his right femur was shattered.

"I know," she sighed. "It's just...I saw enough of you being tortured. I don't want you to go through that again, and I'm guessing that if anyone is an expert at causing pain, Azagoth would be it."

"And you would be right." He brushed a lock of hair back behind her ear, needing an excuse to touch her where Bael had put his filthy mouth. "Lyre?"

"Hmm?"

"What did Bael say to you? You know, right before you did your vapor thing?"

Lyre gave a casual shrug, but he'd seen the look of terror on her face when Bael was bent over her, his teeth grazing her ear.

"Apparently, virgin fallen angels are hard to find," she said. "He and Moloc decided to use me for some kind of mating ceremony to make themselves whole." She shook her head. "I have no idea what that means. Anyway, when Bael sensed that I was no longer 'pure,' he got a little cranky."

"I wish the bastard wasn't dead," he growled. "I want to kill him again."

"Well, there's always Moloc and Flail," she said as she channeled a wave of healing power into him. She'd been sending pulses through him every couple of minutes as her power recharged. He wished he could do the same for her, but there wasn't any guarantee that he'd develop that skill. He couldn't wait for his new wings to find out.

"I'm sure Azagoth will handle Moloc." Flail, however, was his.

The mention of Azagoth's name put a shadow of worry in Lyre's eyes, and he wished he could reassure her, but he wasn't a hundred percent on the likelihood of surviving the rest of the day.

"So who are we going to talk to first?" she asked. "Azagoth? Your friend Hawkyn?"

"I don't know. Whoever we see first, I guess. I have to apologize to everyone. I'm responsible for the death of a child who was the sibling of every Memitim in Sheoul-gra. I owe them all an explanation."

"Okay." She went up on her toes and kissed him, her warm lips giving him the courage to get this done.

Except "getting it done" took longer than expected. The battle with Bael had drained him of power, leaving him with a single drop that was barely enough to interrupt the spell protecting Sheoul-gra's entrance. He was so weakened, in fact, that he couldn't completely bring it down. He could only pause it.

"We have five seconds," he said. "Let's go."

They materialized on the landing pad, and almost immediately, Zhubaal arrived, his expression a storm cloud. Cipher stepped in front of Lyre, putting himself in the path of Azagoth's chief enforcer. No one got to manhandle Lyre but Cipher.

He was about to make that clear when he heard Hawkyn call out his name.

"Cipher!" Hawk charged past Zhubaal and tackled him in a massive bear hug. "You're alive! Fuck me, I didn't think I'd ever see you again." He stepped back and looked him up and down. "Are you evil? Tell me you're not evil. I don't want to have to put you down."

Cipher laughed. "I'm surprisingly myself."

Z watched from the periphery, his hand at his sword hilt, his gaze watchful but non-threatening. He was ready to take Cipher out, but he was trusting Hawkyn to handle the situation.

Cool. Cipher had always liked Zhubaal. The fallen angel had a good head on his shoulders and he was a total dick. What wasn't to like?

Journey, Maddox, Emerico, and Jasmine, a few of Hawkyn's siblings, sprinted toward them, all smiles. Word was spreading fast. It wouldn't be long before Azagoth either sent for him or showed up.

Cipher wasn't sure which would be worse.

Hawkyn shifted his gaze to Lyre. "Ciph's last message said he had inside help to escape Bael's territory. You must be Lyre. I'm Hawkyn."

"It's good to finally meet you," she said. "Cipher has a lot of faith in your friendship."

"Yeah?" Hawkyn looked like he was about to say something that would be completely humiliating to Cipher—because what else were friends for—but the group of loudmouthed Memitim led by Journey stormed the landing pad.

They tackled him the way Hawkyn had, all smiles and "welcome back" and "tell us everything."

And for the first time in months, Cipher truly relaxed.

He was home.

He glanced around, frowning as he realized that shit was a mess. Statues were toppled, pillars smashed, and even a couple of trees were down. Memitim were working to clean up, although several had stopped what they were doing to watch the Cipher Show.

"What happened?"

Maddox jerked his thumb toward Azagoth's mansion. "Pops got into it with Reaver and Revenant."

"Why?"

Jasmine shook her dark head. "Dunno."

"Where is he?" He was almost afraid to ask, and Lyre gave his hand a comforting squeeze.

"Last time I saw him he was with Lilliana," Rico said.

Well, that was interesting. And potentially good news for Azagoth's mood. "I thought Lilliana left him."

"Dude, she's back," Journey said. "Like, last week. And get this, she's pregnant!"

Cipher stared in disbelief. "No. Seriously?"

Hawkyn nodded. "She just showed up one day, nine months pregnant."

Holy shit. "How did your father take it?"

"I've never seen him happier." Hawkyn gestured toward all the destroyed shit. "I mean, you know, as happy as he gets."

"I have a theory." Maddox took an enormous gulp of the soda in his hand. "What if the baby's not his?"

All heads swiveled toward Mad.

"*What?*" That came from everyone.

"Think about it, yo. She was gone nine months. She's nine months pregnant. She could have boned some dude after she left, like she was getting back at him or something, and bam! Preggo. She had to come back so he'd think it was his. You watch. This baby will be 'late.'" He added a wink to the last bit.

Journey scowled at his brother. "You're such a jackass."

"And how." Hawkyn opened his mouth to say something else, but abruptly, the ground shifted and the air went still and cold.

Oh, fuck.

"Uh-oh," Maddox said in a quiet, singsong voice. "Daddy's here."

Cipher shot Hawkyn a look, and Hawk dipped his head in understanding. Knowing his friend would keep Lyre safe, Cipher moved toward Azagoth, a cold knot of anticipation tightening in his chest.

At least he's in his fallen angel suit.

It was a small comfort that Azagoth was striding down the path in black slacks and a matching shirt instead of wearing scales and horns, but Cipher would take what he could get. Especially because, even from twenty paces away, he could see flames dancing in Azagoth's unyielding emerald eyes.

The Grim Reaper was extra grim today.

Adrenaline shot through Cipher as he prepared for whatever Azagoth was going to do to him. In Sheoul-gra, most angelic and demonic abilities were muted or useless, and even if they had been allowed and Cipher was at full strength, he couldn't stand up against the Grim Reaper's awesome power.

Azagoth's boots cracked the pavers as he stopped a mere three feet away, well inside Cipher's comfort zone. Of course, Cipher's comfort zone with Azagoth was three *miles*, not three feet.

Swallowing dryly, Cipher bowed. "My lord—"

"Not. A. Word." Azagoth's voice sounded like it had been filtered through the walls of a coffin. "You're still breathing for one reason. And that reason is Hawkyn."

Of that, Cipher had no doubt. He inclined his head in a respectful nod and looked back, meeting Hawkyn's gaze.

Thank you.

Again Hawkyn gave a solemn nod of acknowledgement before a flash of humor crossed his face and he mouthed, *You owe me.*

A thousand times over, buddy.

"Tell me why you gave the names of my children to my enemy," Azagoth continued, his expression as cold as his eyes were hot. "*Now* you may speak. And be careful. Hawkyn only holds so much sway with me."

Cipher took a deep, bracing breath, and when he spoke, it was with determination, sincerity, and a need to show Azagoth that he wasn't the devil-may-care playboy he used to be, but he was as loyal as he ever was.

"My lord, I'm sorry about your daughter. I'm so sorry." He raised his voice, needing everyone to hear this. "I gave the names of Azagoth's children to Bael in exchange for a chance to escape. I thought I was tricking him. I thought all of those children had already been brought to Sheoul-gra. I didn't know any were still out in the human realm." He met the gaze of every single Memitim before turning back to Azagoth, who stared in silent judgment. "I'm sorry," he repeated, even though it wasn't enough. There weren't enough apologies in the universe for this. "I'd take it back if I could."

"It's true!" Lyre shoved past the ring of Memitim before Hawkyn could grab her. "He didn't know. He was devastated when he found out. He wanted revenge as much as anyone."

"*Not* as much as anyone," Azagoth snapped.

Lyre cursed as Hawk snared her arm and gently reeled her in. "Cipher killed Bael with an *aural* from Bael's own armory."

Azagoth's sharp eyes bored into Cipher. "*You* killed Bael? It wasn't my souls?"

Cipher would have been content to let Azagoth believe that his souls had taken down Bael, but Lyre would have none of it, and she shrugged out of Hawkyn's grip.

"He could have waited for one of your souls to do it," she said boldly. "But he didn't. He wanted Bael to pay for what he'd done."

Cipher swore storm clouds were brewing over Azagoth's head. "Who *are* you?"

"My lord," Cipher said, moving to intercept, "this is Lyre. She helped me escape, and if not for her, Bael wouldn't be dead." He turned to her, awed by her bravery. She might claim to have weak powers, but she was a warrior from the tips of her wings to the depths of her heart. "And if she'll have me, I would have her as my mate."

Lyre's eyes flared, her mouth fell open, and he nearly groaned. Was it too soon? What if she rejected him in front of all his friends? What if she rejected him *anywhere*? He was alive because of her. He wasn't drenched in evil because of her. He was home because of her.

He owed her everything, and he'd already given her the one thing he never thought he'd surrender.

His heart.

"Yes," she whispered. "I would love to be your mate."

Relief and elation left him momentarily frozen, but once his feet could move again he gathered her in his arms. He wanted to celebrate properly, but it could wait.

Azagoth wouldn't.

Cipher kissed her, a peck with a promise of more later, and turned back to Azagoth. "Lyre didn't have to help me, but she did. When she learned all that Bael and Moloc planned to do, including murdering your children, she turned against them."

Azagoth's gemstone eyes once again flashed with intensity, but when he spoke, the razor edge in his voice had dulled. "The daughter on the list, my daughter who died...she was part of a plan. I can accept that. I don't like it, but it's beyond my ability to change. Prove to me Amelia didn't die in vain."

"I will," Cipher vowed. "I swear."

Silence stretched, a make-'em-sweat tactic Azagoth had trademarked. "Hawkyn insists you'll be an asset to Sheoul-gra," he finally said. "Time will tell. But if you do anything, and I mean *anything*, to make me regret this..." Azagoth paused, his lips peeled back from deadly fangs. "I don't need to go on, do I?"

"No, sir, I'd rather you didn't."

With a hint of a smile and a nod so shallow Cipher questioned whether it happened at all, Azagoth flashed away, leaving him with all he'd ever wanted.

His home, his friends, and now, Lyre.

Chapter Twenty-Four

Life inside Sheoul-gra turned out to not be horrible.

Cipher was right: his friends were decent people, and while many of the Memitim were a little chilly toward her, she couldn't blame them. She and Cipher were fallen angels with a history of working for one of the worst overlords Sheoul had to offer, and given the recent murder within Sheoul-gra's borders, trust didn't come easily.

But she was willing to do what it took to gain that trust. Azagoth was going to be a hard sell, and frankly, she chose to just avoid him when possible. Bael had been terrifying, but the Grim Reaper made him look like a kitten in comparison.

Cipher had gone straight to work for Azagoth, hacking into enemy computers. Once his wings grew in and his powers were restored, Azagoth said he'd make use of his spell-coding skills, as well. At least his ability to flash had come back, so things were moving along.

Lyre...she wasn't sure where she'd fit in yet. Her powers were so weak she feared she'd never get a job, but just this morning, one week after escaping Bael's clutches, Azagoth came to her with a proposal. She'd listened in silent terror as he explained that her lack of strong abilities had the potential to make her all but invisible to power-sensing demons in the Inner Sanctum, and in addition to using her for intel into Bael and Moloc's methods, he had some spy work for her. Her gift of turning into a wisp of vapor would give her even more ways to ensure she went undetected.

She could do that. It sounded fun, actually.

And as she was sitting in their apartment inside Sheoul-gra, reading up on everything she could find about the Inner Sanctum, Cipher offered her a break.

"I have a surprise for you," he said, taking her hand and pulling her up from the sofa.

She beamed. "Really?"

"I'm not sure it's a good surprise," he hedged, "but it might be what you need."

Uh-oh. That didn't sound great. Sounded terrible, in fact. "So where do we have to go for this unnecessary surprise?"

"I'll show you."

He escorted her to the portal, where they dematerialized and re-formed at the earthly forest clearing they'd used when they'd first entered Sheoul. Once topside, he flashed them to a dusty hilltop in Israel, and she cursed. Megiddo. He'd brought her to a place of angelic importance. Where executions and battles and expulsions from Heaven had taken place.

"What the hell is this, Cipher? Why are we here?"

A hot wind spun up, and a split-second later, Lihandra materialized alongside Lyre's other sister, Bellagias.

Anger, as hot as the wind, blasted her, but the funny thing was that she didn't experience the murderous rage she'd felt for years while she was in Sheoul. This was just good old-fashioned pissed.

"I asked Hawkyn to contact your family," Cipher said. "I hope that's okay."

It wasn't, but she nodded anyway. "It's good to see you, Bella." All she could muster for Lihandra was a glare.

Bella, always a softie, threw herself at Lyre, wrapping her arms around her in an enormous hug. "I'm so glad you're okay. I've been so worried about you."

Lyre pulled back. "Really?"

She nodded. "Mother and Father, too. And, believe it or not, Liha."

Lyre laughed, but when she looked over at her other sister, Lihandra's expression was serious. "I'm having a hard time believing that."

"I wouldn't be here if it wasn't true," Lihandra said. "I...regret what I did."

Lyre could have been knocked over by one of Lihandra's lacy ivory feathers. "Seriously?"

"I could have handled it better," she admitted. "I don't regret the demon's death, but you shouldn't have lost your wings."

Ah, well, that was more like it. Anger steamed through her again, but when she glanced over at Cipher, his calm, strong presence brought her down. Nothing from her past mattered anymore. Holding this grudge wouldn't hurt her sister; it would hurt only her, and possibly her relationship with the male she loved.

She had to let it go.

"I forgive you, Lihandra," she said, and it was her sister's turn to be shocked. "But I don't want to see you again. Not for a while. Maybe not ever."

"What kind of forgiveness is that?" Lihandra said in a clipped, stung voice.

"Considering that just a week ago I wanted you dead, I figure it's a pretty huge development. I'm sorry, did you *want* a relationship with me?" Lihandra's mouth opened. Closed. Yeah, that's what Lyre thought. As usual, she was playing the wronged party, but this time she got called out on her fake outrage. "I didn't think so. Let's just walk away from this with a fresh start. Agreed?"

Lihandra bowed her head. "Since I'm no longer welcome in your presence, I'll go. Take care, sister."

With that, Lihandra launched into the sky and flashed away.

"She's such a bitch," Bella said. "But I should go too. Call me and we'll do lunch sometime."

She and her sister used to *do lunch* all the time, and Lyre truly hoped her sister was sincere. Especially because now that Lyre was no longer bound to Bael's realm, she could flash anywhere she wanted to inside the demon and human realms.

They'd just have to keep their lunches secret. While it wasn't strictly forbidden for a Heavenly angel to have lunch with a fallen angel, it was a reputation-killer.

She waved as Bella lifted off, and then she turned to Cipher, who watched with what looked like envy. It could take months to regrow wings, and until then, he'd be earthbound. Maybe she could keep him distracted. With sex. Yep, that sounded like a plan.

"That was the nicest thing anyone has done for me in a long time," she said.

He shrugged as if it was no big deal, but it was. It *so* was. "After all those years of wanting revenge, I thought you might need some closure."

She flew into his strong arms, her heart singing. "You're amazing. I love you so much."

Emotion poured out of her as she held onto Cipher, and her wings erupted of their own accord, surrounding them in the most intimate of angelic embraces.

Swallowing a lump of his own emotion, he traced the edge of a wing with his finger. "I love you too." Tenderly, he pressed a kiss into her hair. "And now I have a favor to ask of you."

"Of course," she said. "Anything."

Shadows of hesitation danced in his eyes before he blurted, "Someday we'll have kids, right?"

She hadn't really thought that far ahead, but yes, she absolutely wanted to have Cipher's babies. Lots of them. "I can't see why not."

His lips curved into a happy smile, but his eyes remained shadowed. "If we have a girl, and it's all right with Azagoth, I'd like to name her Amelia. Would that be okay?"

"Oh, yes," she whispered. "What a wonderful tribute to Azagoth's daughter." And what an incredible male he was to want to honor her that way. How had Lyre gotten so lucky? She held him tighter, putting their hearts together. "Thank you, Cipher. Thank you for hacking my password and rebooting my system."

He laughed at the computer reference and pulled back just enough to look down at her, his gorgeous eyes mirroring the joy she felt. "I can say the same about you. I can even thank Flail. If she hadn't gotten me abducted, I never would have found you or discovered my unique power."

She wondered where Flail had gone after the torture box had opened. Who was she working for now? And was she going to seek revenge? The female would be crazy to attempt it, but she'd never struck Lyre as all that stable. They were going to have to be on guard.

Lyre playfully drummed her fingers on Cipher's chest. "So Flail's forgiven?"

The dark, deadly smile tipping up one corner of his mouth gave her delicious shivers. "Oh, I'm still going to kill her. But I'll thank her before I do."

"That's my evil boy," she teased.

But really, the good/evil battle they both were facing as True Fallens was something everyone, from demons to humans to angels, had to endure on a daily basis. It was part of life, and there was a reason for it. There was a reason for everything, and for the first time in years, she believed that again.

She believed in a lot of things again.

Epilogue

Moloc stared out the window at the glorious scorched earth and burning corpses that surrounded his stronghold. One would think there had been a battle, but it had been better than that.

The explosion of his soul merging with Bael's had caused a catastrophic blast he still felt inside him. And oh, it was good.

He was whole for the first time in his life.

He and Bael had always had a strange relationship, knowing that they were both brothers and a single person, and he'd wondered how it would feel when they were finally melded together inside one body.

Now he knew. It felt like power.

He reached for the vial next to him, a vial he'd been saving for thousands of years. A gift from Satan himself, the little glass tube contained the Dark Lord's blood, meant to strengthen him and, he hoped, give him a psychic connection with his king.

As he brought it to his lips, there was a tap at the door. The chaotic half of his soul that had been Bael wanted to strike out at the interruption, but the calm half, the one Moloc had possessed, overruled.

"Come in," he said, but added for Bael, "but if you displease me, you die."

The door swung open and Flail strutted in, a smile on her usually pouty lips. "I have news from our agent inside Sheoul-gra."

"I'm listening."

"Cipher and Lyre are there," she growled. "Azagoth has accepted them."

"Disappointing, but not entirely unexpected," he said. "What about his young human-realm children?"

"They've all been taken to Sheoul-gra. We won't be able to kill more of them."

He smiled. "No matter. I have a new a plan. One that is guaranteed to force the Keeper of Souls to release Satan from prison."

"You won't be able to kidnap Lilliana," she warned. "Not even with your insider. She's guarded all the time."

"That's the beauty of it, my love," he said, Bael's influence already affecting his choice of words. "I won't need to abduct her."

"Why not?" Confusion pulled her brow down. "I don't understand."

That was because she was beautiful but not all that bright. Females never were.

"Because," he said, his heart racing with anticipation, "when the time is right, Lilliana will come to me, and Azagoth will be mine."

* * * *

Coming October 15, 2019 from 1001 Dark Nights and Larissa Ione:

REAPER: A Demonica Novel

THE DEMONICA SERIES RETURNS...

He is the Keeper of Souls. Judge, jury, and executioner. He is death personified.

He is the Grim Reaper.

A fallen angel who commands the respect of both Heaven and Hell, Azagoth has presided over his own underworld realm for thousands of years. As the overlord of evil souls, he maintains balance crucial to the existence of life on Earth and beyond. But as all the realms gear up for the prophesied End of Days, the ties that bind him to Sheoul-gra have begun to chafe.

Now, with his beloved mate and unborn child the target of an ancient enemy, Azagoth will stop at nothing to save them, even if it means breaking blood oaths and shattering age-old alliances.

Even if it means destroying himself and setting the world on fire...

Sign up for the 1001 Dark Nights Newsletter
and be entered to win a Tiffany Key necklace.

There's a contest every month!

Go to www.1001DarkNights.com to subscribe.

**As a bonus, all subscribers can download
FIVE FREE exclusive books!**

Discover 1001 Dark Nights Collection Six

Go to www.1001DarkNights.com for more information.

DRAGON CLAIMED by Donna Grant
A Dark Kings Novella

ASHES TO INK by Carrie Ann Ryan
A Montgomery Ink: Colorado Springs Novella

ENSNARED by Elisabeth Naughton
An Eternal Guardians Novella

EVERMORE by Corinne Michaels
A Salvation Series Novella

VENGEANCE by Rebecca Zanetti
A Dark Protectors/Rebels Novella

ELI'S TRIUMPH by Joanna Wylde
A Reapers MC Novella

CIPHER by Larissa Ione
A Demonica Underworld Novella

RESCUING MACIE by Susan Stoker
A Delta Force Heroes Novella

ENCHANTED by Lexi Blake
A Masters and Mercenaries Novella

TAKE THE BRIDE by Carly Phillips
A Knight Brothers Novella

INDULGE ME by J. Kenner
A Stark Ever After Novella

THE KING by Jennifer L. Armentrout
A Wicked Novella

QUIET MAN by Kristen Ashley
A Dream Man Novella

ABANDON by Rachel Van Dyken
A Seaside Pictures Novella

THE OPEN DOOR by Laurelin Paige
A Found Duet Novella

CLOSER by Kylie Scott
A Stage Dive Novella

SOMETHING JUST LIKE THIS by Jennifer Probst
A Stay Novella

BLOOD NIGHT by Heather Graham
A Krewe of Hunters Novella

TWIST OF FATE by Jill Shalvis
A Heartbreaker Bay Novella

MORE THAN PLEASURE YOU by Shayla Black
A More Than Words Novella

WONDER WITH ME by Kristen Proby
A With Me In Seattle Novella

THE DARKEST ASSASSIN by Gena Showalter
A Lords of the Underworld Novella

Also from 1001 Dark Nights:
DAMIEN by J. Kenner

Discover 1001 Dark Nights

COLLECTION ONE
FOREVER WICKED by Shayla Black
CRIMSON TWILIGHT by Heather Graham
CAPTURED IN SURRENDER by Liliana Hart
SILENT BITE: A SCANGUARDS WEDDING by Tina Folsom
DUNGEON GAMES by Lexi Blake
AZAGOTH by Larissa Ione
NEED YOU NOW by Lisa Renee Jones
SHOW ME, BABY by Cherise Sinclair
ROPED IN by Lorelei James
TEMPTED BY MIDNIGHT by Lara Adrian
THE FLAME by Christopher Rice
CARESS OF DARKNESS by Julie Kenner

COLLECTION TWO
WICKED WOLF by Carrie Ann Ryan
WHEN IRISH EYES ARE HAUNTING by Heather Graham
EASY WITH YOU by Kristen Proby
MASTER OF FREEDOM by Cherise Sinclair
CARESS OF PLEASURE by Julie Kenner
ADORED by Lexi Blake
HADES by Larissa Ione
RAVAGED by Elisabeth Naughton
DREAM OF YOU by Jennifer L. Armentrout
STRIPPED DOWN by Lorelei James
RAGE/KILLIAN by Alexandra Ivy/Laura Wright
DRAGON KING by Donna Grant
PURE WICKED by Shayla Black
HARD AS STEEL by Laura Kaye
STROKE OF MIDNIGHT by Lara Adrian
ALL HALLOWS EVE by Heather Graham
KISS THE FLAME by Christopher Rice
DARING HER LOVE by Melissa Foster
TEASED by Rebecca Zanetti
THE PROMISE OF SURRENDER by Liliana Hart

COLLECTION THREE

HIDDEN INK by Carrie Ann Ryan
BLOOD ON THE BAYOU by Heather Graham
SEARCHING FOR MINE by Jennifer Probst
DANCE OF DESIRE by Christopher Rice
ROUGH RHYTHM by Tessa Bailey
DEVOTED by Lexi Blake
Z by Larissa Ione
FALLING UNDER YOU by Laurelin Paige
EASY FOR KEEPS by Kristen Proby
UNCHAINED by Elisabeth Naughton
HARD TO SERVE by Laura Kaye
DRAGON FEVER by Donna Grant
KAYDEN/SIMON by Alexandra Ivy/Laura Wright
STRUNG UP by Lorelei James
MIDNIGHT UNTAMED by Lara Adrian
TRICKED by Rebecca Zanetti
DIRTY WICKED by Shayla Black
THE ONLY ONE by Lauren Blakely
SWEET SURRENDER by Liliana Hart

COLLECTION FOUR
ROCK CHICK REAWAKENING by Kristen Ashley
ADORING INK by Carrie Ann Ryan
SWEET RIVALRY by K. Bromberg
SHADE'S LADY by Joanna Wylde
RAZR by Larissa Ione
ARRANGED by Lexi Blake
TANGLED by Rebecca Zanetti
HOLD ME by J. Kenner
SOMEHOW, SOME WAY by Jennifer Probst
TOO CLOSE TO CALL by Tessa Bailey
HUNTED by Elisabeth Naughton
EYES ON YOU by Laura Kaye
BLADE by Alexandra Ivy/Laura Wright
DRAGON BURN by Donna Grant
TRIPPED OUT by Lorelei James
STUD FINDER by Lauren Blakely
MIDNIGHT UNLEASHED by Lara Adrian
HALLOW BE THE HAUNT by Heather Graham

DIRTY FILTHY FIX by Laurelin Paige
THE BED MATE by Kendall Ryan
NIGHT GAMES by CD Reiss
NO RESERVATIONS by Kristen Proby
DAWN OF SURRENDER by Liliana Hart

COLLECTION FIVE
BLAZE ERUPTING by Rebecca Zanetti
ROUGH RIDE by Kristen Ashley
HAWKYN by Larissa Ione
RIDE DIRTY by Laura Kaye
ROME'S CHANCE by Joanna Wylde
THE MARRIAGE ARRANGEMENT by Jennifer Probst
SURRENDER by Elisabeth Naughton
INKED NIGHTS by Carrie Ann Ryan
ENVY by Rachel Van Dyken
PROTECTED by Lexi Blake
THE PRINCE by Jennifer L. Armentrout
PLEASE ME by J. Kenner
WOUND TIGHT by Lorelei James
STRONG by Kylie Scott
DRAGON NIGHT by Donna Grant
TEMPTING BROOKE by Kristen Proby
HAUNTED BE THE HOLIDAYS by Heather Graham
CONTROL by K. Bromberg
HUNKY HEARTBREAKER by Kendall Ryan
THE DARKEST CAPTIVE by Gena Showalter

Also from 1001 Dark Nights:

TAME ME by J. Kenner
THE SURRENDER GATE By Christopher Rice
SERVICING THE TARGET By Cherise Sinclair
TEMPT ME by J. Kenner

Discover More Larissa Ione

Dining with Angels: Bits & Bites from the Demonica Universe by Larissa Ione, Recipes by Suzanne M. Johnson

In a world where humans and supernatural beings coexist — not always peacefully — three things can bring everyone to the table: Love, a mutual enemy, and, of course, food.

With seven brand new stories from the Demonica universe, New York Times bestselling author Larissa Ione has the love and enemies covered, while celebrity Southern food expert Suzanne Johnson brings delicious food to the party.

And who doesn't love a party? (Harvester rolls her eyes and raises her hand, but we know she's lying.)

Join Ares and Cara as they celebrate a new addition to their family. See what Reaver and Harvester are doing to "spice" things up. Find out what trouble Reseph might have gotten himself into with Jillian. You'll love reading about the further adventures of Wraith and Serena, Declan and Suzanne, and Shade and Runa, and you're not going to want to miss the sit down with Eidolon and Tayla.

So pour a glass of the Grim Reaper's finest wine and settle in for slices of life from your favorite characters and the recipes that bring them together. Whether you're dining with angels, drinking with demons, or hanging with humans, you'll find the perfect heavenly bits and sinful bites to suit the occasion.

Happy reading and happy eating!

* * * *

Her Guardian Angel: A Demonica Underworld/Masters and Mercenaries Novella by Larissa Ione

After a difficult childhood and a turbulent stint in the military, Declan Burke finally got his act together. Now he's a battle-hardened professional bodyguard who takes his job at McKay-Taggart seriously and his playtime – and his play*mates* – just as seriously. One thing he never does, however, is mix business with pleasure. But when the mysterious, gorgeous Suzanne D'Angelo needs his protection from a stalker, his desire for her burns out of control, tempting him to break all the rules…even as he's drawn into a dark, dangerous world he didn't know existed.

Suzanne is an earthbound angel on her critical first mission: protecting Declan from an emerging supernatural threat at all costs. To keep him close, she hires him as her bodyguard. It doesn't take long for her to realize that she's in over her head, defenseless against this devastatingly sexy human who makes her crave his forbidden touch.

Together they'll have to draw on every ounce of their collective training to resist each other as the enemy closes in, but soon it becomes apparent that nothing could have prepared them for the menace to their lives…or their hearts.

* * * *

Razr: A Demonica Novella by Larissa Ione

A fallen angel with a secret.
An otherworldly elf with an insatiable hunger she doesn't understand.
An enchanted gem.
Meet mortal enemies Razr and Jedda…and the priceless diamond that threatens to destroy them both even as it bonds them together with sizzling passion.

Welcome back to the Demonica Underworld, where enemies find love…if they're strong enough to survive.

* * * *

Z: A Demonica Underworld Novella by Larissa Ione

Zhubaal, fallen angel assistant to the Grim Reaper, has spent decades searching for the angel he loved and lost nearly a century ago. Not even her death can keep him from trying to find her, not when he knows she's been given a second chance at life in a new body. But as time passes, he's losing hope, and he wonders how much longer he can hold to the oath he swore to her so long ago…

As an *emim*, the wingless offspring of two fallen angels, Vex has always felt like a second-class citizen. But if she manages to secure a deal with the Grim Reaper — by any means necessary — she will have earned her place in the world. The only obstacle in the way of her plan is a sexy hardass called Z, who seems determined to thwart her at every turn. Soon it becomes clear that they have a powerful connection rooted in the past...but can any vow stand the test of time?

* * * *

Hades: A Demonica Underworld Novella by Larissa Ione

A fallen angel with a mean streak and a mohawk, Hades has spent thousands of years serving as Jailor of the Underworld. The souls he guards are as evil as they come, but few dare to cross him. All of that changes when a sexy fallen angel infiltrates his prison and unintentionally starts a riot. It's easy enough to quell an uprising, but for the first time, Hades is torn between delivering justice — or bestowing mercy — on the beautiful female who could be his salvation...or his undoing.

Thanks to her unwitting participation in another angel's plot to start Armageddon, Cataclysm was kicked out of Heaven and is now a fallen angel in service of Hades's boss, Azagoth. All she wants is to redeem herself and get back where she belongs. But when she gets trapped in Hades's prison domain with only the cocky but irresistible Hades to help her, Cat finds that where she belongs might be in the place she least expected...

* * * *

Azagoth: A Demonica Underword Novella by Larissa Ione

Even in the fathomless depths of the underworld and the bleak chambers of a damaged heart, the bonds of love can heal...or destroy.

He holds the ability to annihilate souls in the palm of his hand. He commands the respect of the most dangerous of demons and the most powerful of angels. He can seduce and dominate any female he wants with a mere look. But for all Azagoth's power, he's bound by shackles of his own making, and only an angel with a secret holds the key to his release.

She's an angel with the extraordinary ability to travel through time and space. An angel with a tormented past she can't escape. And when Lilliana is sent to Azagoth's underworld realm, she finds that her past isn't all she can't escape. For the irresistibly sexy fallen angel known as Azagoth is also known as the Grim Reaper, and when he claims a soul, it's forever…

Dining with Angels
Bits & Bites from the Demonica Universe
By Larissa Ione, Recipes by Suzanne M. Johnson

In a world where humans and supernatural beings coexist — not always peacefully — three things can bring everyone to the table: Love, a mutual enemy, and, of course, food.

With seven brand new stories from the Demonica universe, New York Times bestselling author Larissa Ione has the love and enemies covered, while celebrity Southern food expert Suzanne Johnson brings delicious food to the party.

And who doesn't love a party? (Harvester rolls her eyes and raises her hand, but we know she's lying.)

Join Ares and Cara as they celebrate a new addition to their family. See what Reaver and Harvester are doing to "spice" things up. Find out what trouble Reseph might have gotten himself into with Jillian. You'll love reading about the further adventures of Wraith and Serena, Declan and Suzanne, and Shade and Runa, and you're not going to want to miss the sit down with Eidolon and Tayla.

So pour a glass of the Grim Reaper's finest wine and settle in for slices of life from your favorite characters and the recipes that bring them together. Whether you're dining with angels, drinking with demons, or hanging with humans, you'll find the perfect heavenly bits and sinful bites to suit the occasion.

Happy reading and happy eating!

* * * *

The rich, sweet aroma of vanilla made Runa's mouth water as she turned on the professional quality electric mixer her mate, Shade, had gotten her for Christmas. She wasn't a big fan of cooking meals, but she did enjoy baking sweet treats, and her family didn't complain a bit.

Boots clomped on the floor down the hall, and she turned off the mixer as Shade sauntered into the kitchen. He'd donned his black paramedic uniform for his afternoon shift at Underworld General Hospital, and she had a powerful urge to rip it off. Right here in the kitchen. She could finish making cookies to go with the smoothie pops she'd just put in the freezer to celebrate Stryke's A+ in science class later.

"Where are the boys?" he asked as he reached for a bottle of water in the fridge.

"They're at Stewie's pool party. Serena just sent a picture of them playing on the big float. It's on my phone if you want to see it."

"We should get a pool," he said as he swiped his finger across her phone's screen.

"We're welcome to use theirs anytime," she pointed out.

A smile ruffled his lips at the sight of the three dark-haired, espresso-eyed boys, the spitting images of their father, splashing in the water.

"Wraith and Serena made their house *the* place to be when they put it in, didn't they?"

It was probably the very reason they put in the pool. "Well, they love parties and kids."

"That's because they only have one," he muttered, but he was joking. Shade adored children, and when they were around, he could always be found nearby.

She fetched a can of cooking spray from a cupboard. "Speaking of kids, this morning a witch at the hospital told me I'm going to have twins in exactly eight years."

"Only twins?" Shade twisted the cap off his water. "Awesome."

She shook a spatula at him. "I remember when you wanted a whole bunch of kids."

"I remember too," Shade said. "And then we had triplets."

"Are you saying you don't want more?"

Pausing with the bottle at his lips, he shrugged. "We've got centuries ahead of us. I'm not in a hurry."

Neither was she. She loved being a mother, but she only had so much time between volunteering at the hospital and taking care of triplets, a mate, and two homes. Granted, one of the homes was a cave in a jungle, but it still had modern appliances and conveniences like hot running water and toilets, and modern things needed to be cleaned.

"I still can't believe your drive to impregnate me hasn't kicked in since the boys were born."

"That's how it works when we're mated." He grabbed a granola bar from the pantry and tucked it into the leg pocket of his BDU pants. "The drive only kicks in when our mates are ready. You're clearly not ready."

"You think? I barely have time to shower, let alone have more kids.

But I'm sure everything will be different in eight years," she added, with more than a little sarcasm.

"You never know." He waggled his brows. "Wanna practice making our twins?"

Always up for a little practice, Runa eyed her mate, her body already heating at the thought of watching him strip out of his uniform. Or maybe she'd make him leave it on. It was sexy as hell.

"Don't you have to be at work in fifteen minutes?" she asked.

"Con will cover for me. Sin's working late with DART today."

Smiling, she peeled off her shirt and tossed it at him. "Then by all means...let's get some practice in."

About Larissa Ione

Air Force veteran Larissa Ione traded in a career as a meteorologist to pursue her passion of writing. She has since published dozens of books, hit several bestseller lists, including the New York Times and USA Today, and has been nominated for a RITA award. She now spends her days in pajamas with her computer, strong coffee, and fictional worlds. She believes in celebrating everything, and would never be caught without a bottle of Champagne chilling in the fridge…just in case. After a dozen moves all over the country with her now-retired U.S. Coast Guard spouse, she is now settled in Wisconsin with her husband, her teenage son, a rescue cat named Vegas, and her very own hellhounds, a King Shepherd named Hexe, and a Belgian Malinois named Duvel.

For more information about Larissa, visit www.larissaione.com.

On behalf of 1001 Dark Nights,

Liz Berry and M.J. Rose would like to thank ~

Steve Berry
Doug Scofield
Kim Guidroz
Jillian Stein
InkSlinger PR
Dan Slater
Asha Hossain
Chris Graham
Fedora Chen
Kasi Alexander
Jessica Johns
Dylan Stockton
Richard Blake
and Simon Lipskar

56645276R00117

Made in the USA
Columbia, SC
29 April 2019